Stories for Eight-Year-Olds

Stories for
Eight-Year-Olds

and other young readers

------------------------------- * -------------------------------

edited by

SARA AND
STEPHEN CORRIN

illustrated by
SHIRLEY HUGHES

Faber and Faber Limited
London . Boston

First published in 1971
by Faber and Faber Limited
3 Queen Square London WC1
Reprinted 1972, 1974, 1977 and 1980
Unwin Brothers Limited
The Gresham Press, Old Woking, Surrey
All rights reserved

ISBN 0 571 09332 9

Contents

———————————*———————————

Contents

Acknowledgements

————————*————————

We are most grateful to the undermentioned publishers, authors and agents for permission to include the following stories:

Faber and Faber Ltd. for *Little Claus and Big Claus* and *The Nightingale* from *Hans Andersen: Forty-Two Stories*, translated by M. R. James.

John Farquharson Ltd. for *Melisande* by E. Nesbit.

Jonathan Cape Ltd. for *A Chinese Fairy Tale* from *Moonshine and Clover* by Laurence Housman.

Mrs. James Thurber for *Many Moons*. Copyright 1943 James Thurber. Published by Harcourt, Brace and World, Inc.

The Society of Authors as the literary representative of the estate of Rose Fyleman for *The Crocodile and the Monkey* from *Folk-Tales from Many Lands* by Rose Fyleman.

The Literary Trustees of Walter de la Mare and the Society of Authors as their representative for *The Goose-Girl* from *Animal Stories* by Walter de la Mare.

Barbara Leonie Picard for *Gawaine and the Green Knight* from *The Stories of King Arthur and his Knights* published by the Oxford University Press.

Mrs. George Bambridge and Macmillan and Co. Ltd., publishers of *The Jungle Book*, for 'Rikki-Tikki-Tavi' by Rudyard Kipling.

9

Acknowledgements

We should like to thank Miss M. B. McBride, Librarian in charge of work with young people, Barnet Libraries; Mrs. A. Fleet, Children's Librarian at Westminster City Library; and Mrs. S. Stonebridge, Principal Children's Librarian, Royal Borough of Kensington and Chelsea, for their willing and most valuable help; and Miss Phyllis Hunt of Faber and Faber for her advice and encouragement.

A Word to the Story-teller

———————————————————*———————————————————

The welcome given to our *Stories for Six-Year-Olds* and *Stories for Seven-Year-Olds* has encouraged us to add a third volume to the series.

Eight-year-olds need heroes, real or imaginary, who perform great deeds on the grand scale, heroes who overcome all obstacles and make the tyrant and bully grovel in the dust, emerging triumphant in the end. Epic tales of heroic deeds such as these are the very stuff of myth and legend. So deep a need do they fill that many of them were accepted as true, so that, over the generations, they have become part of man's cultural heritage.

The reader may doubt whether stories can be so rigidly classified as to justify the title *Stories for Eight-Year-Olds*. Most teachers will agree that they can, which does not imply, of course, that the same stories will not be of interest to other age groups. It means simply that every age has differing emotional and intellectual requirements and that some stories are very much more suited than others to meet these requirements. Each age-range (and each child within this range) will draw from the story at different levels, according to need; so that in a class of forty eight-year-olds one is catering for forty individuals at forty different levels. And yet the whole class will sit entranced, linked by some magic spell.

The present volume contains a nice mixture of the mythical,

the legendary and the more recent. There is also a liberal sprinkling of humour. The collection has been tried out and proved its worth with classes of eight-years-olds—as well as with individual children. It is a great help if the teacher reads the stories in such a way as to convey her own enthusiasm for them to the child. This goes for the parent, too, as well as for the aunt or elder sister. The story-teller should not be afraid of adding a little trimming here and there. Sometimes a word or phrase may be adapted to suit the capacity or temperament of the particular listener. And above all, the story-teller must not fight shy of dramatizing—dramatic tension is the one thing which young people find irresistible. All this is safely within the story-telling tradition, for over the many years that traditional tales have been handed down they have been added to and embellished in all sorts of ways. But never, of course, beyond recognition. The basic themes remain; we find them appearing in various guises in all parts of the world.

Little Claus and Big Claus

———————————✳———————————

There were two men in a town, who both had the same name, both were called Claus; but one of them owned four horses, and the other only one. Now, in order to be able to tell one from the other, people called the one who had four horses Big Claus, and the one who had only one horse Little Claus. Now we must hear how these two got on, for it makes a regular story.

All the week through, Little Claus had to plough for Big Claus, and lend him his one horse; and in return Big Claus used to help him with all his four horses, but only once a week, and that was on the Sunday. Hurrah! how Little Claus did crack his whip over all the five horses, that were as good as his own for that one day. The sun shone bright, and all the bells in the church tower rang for church, and the people were dressed out and going past with their hymn books under their arms to hear the clergyman preach; and they looked at Little Claus ploughing away with five horses, and he was so pleased, he cracked his whip again and called out, "Hup, all my horses!"

"You mustn't say that," said Big Claus, "it's only one horse that's yours."

But again, when somebody else went by going to church, Little Claus forgot that he wasn't to say that, and he called out, "Hup, all my horses!"

"Now then, I'll ask you kindly to leave off," said Big Claus. "For if you say that once more I shall knock your horse on the head, so that it'll die on the spot, and that'll be the end of it."

"To be sure, I won't say it any more," said Little Claus. But when some people went by and nodded him good morning, he was delighted; and he thought it looked so fine, his having five horses to plough his field with, that he cracked his whip and called out, "Hup, all my horses!"

"I'll hup your horses," said Big Claus, and he took the tether-peg mallet and hit Little Claus's only horse on the forehead, so that it tumbled down quite dead.

"Oh! now I haven't got any horse at all!" said Little Claus, and began to cry. Later on he flayed the horse, took the hide and let it dry well in the open air, and then stuffed it into a bag which he put on his back, and went off to the town to sell his horse-hide.

He had a long way to go, which took him through a large dark forest, and there a terrible storm came on and he quite lost himself, and before he could find the right road, it was evening, and too late to get either to the town or home again before night fell.

Hard by the road there stood a big farmhouse. The shutters outside were closed in front of the windows, but still the light shone out at the top of them. "I expect I can get leave to stay there for the night," thought Little Claus, and he went and knocked at the door.

The farmer's wife opened the door, but when she heard what he wanted, she told him to go along: her husband wasn't at home and she wouldn't take in any strangers.

"Oh, well then, I must lie out of doors," said Little Claus, and the farmer's wife shut the door in his face.

Close by there stood a large haystack, and between it and the house a little shed had been built, with a flat roof of thatch.

"I can lie up there," said Little Claus when he saw the roof.

"It makes a beautiful bed. I don't suppose the stork will fly down and peck my legs"; for there was a live stork up on the roof, where it had its nest.

So Little Claus climbed up on the shed, and there he lay down, and rolled about in order to lie comfortably. The wooden shutters in front of the windows did not reach up to the top of them; so he could look right into the room. There was a big table laid out with wine and a roast joint, and such a splendid fish! The farmer's wife and the parish clerk were sitting at table, and nobody else; and she helped him to wine, and he helped himself to fish; a thing he was very fond of.

"If only one could get some of that!" said Little Claus, and poked his head right close to the window. Gracious! what a beautiful cake he could see in there! Really it was a feast.

Just then he heard someone coming, riding along the high road towards the house. It was the woman's husband coming home.

He was an excellent man, but he had this very odd ailment, that he could never bear to see a parish clerk; if he caught sight of a parish clerk he went quite mad with rage, and this was why the clerk had come in to say how-do-you-do to the woman, because he knew her husband wasn't at home; and so the kind woman had got out all the best victuals she had for him. But now when they heard the husband coming they were terribly frightened, and the woman begged the clerk to creep into a great empty chest that stood in the corner; and so he did, for he knew well enough that the poor husband couldn't bear to see parish clerks. The woman made haste to hide all the good victuals and the wine in her oven, for if her husband had caught sight of them he would have been certain to ask what it all meant.

"Ah dear!" sighed Little Claus on the top of the shed, when he saw all the victuals taken away. "Is there somebody up there?" asked the farmer, and looked up at Little Claus. "What are you lying up there for? Better come indoors with me."

Then Little Claus told him how he had lost his way, and asked if he might stay for the night.

"Yes, to be sure," said the farmer, "but first we must have a bit to eat."

The wife greeted them very friendly, both of them, and spread a long table and gave them a large dish of porridge. The farmer was hungry and ate with a fine appetite, but Little Claus couldn't help thinking about the beautiful roast joint and fish and cake, which he knew were there in the oven. He had laid his sack with the horse's hide in it under the table beside his feet; we remember, of course, that that was what he had come away from home with, to sell it in the town. He had no taste for the porridge, and so he trod on his bag and the dry hide in the sack squeaked quite loud.

"Hush," said Little Claus to his sack; but at the same moment he trod on it again, and it squeaked much louder than before.

"Why, what have you got in your bag?" asked the farmer. "Oh, that's a wizard," said Little Claus. "He's saying that we mustn't eat porridge, for he's conjured the whole oven full of roast meat and fish and cake."

"What's that?" said the farmer, and in a trice opened the oven and saw in it all the good victuals which his wife had hidden there, but which—as he thought—the wizard in the bag had conjured into it. His wife durstn't say anything, but put the food on the table at once, and so they had their fill of the fish and the joint and the cake. Directly after, Little Claus trod on his bag again and made the hide speak.

"What's he saying now?" asked the farmer. "He's saying," said Little Claus, "that he's also conjured us up three bottles of wine, and they are in the oven too." Then the wife had to bring out the wine she had hidden, and the farmer drank and got quite merry. Such a wizard as Little Claus had in the bag he would dearly like to have.

"Can he call up the devil, too?" asked the farmer. "I'd like to see him, for I'm in spirits now."

"Yes," said Little Claus, "my wizard can do anything I require. Can't you?" he asked, and he trod on the bag and it squeaked. "D'you hear? he says 'Yes'. But the devil is very ugly to look at, and I wouldn't trouble about seeing him."

"Oh, I'm not a bit afraid. What do you suppose he looks like?"

"Why, he'll show himself for all the world like a parish clerk."

"Ugh!" said the farmer, "that is horrid; you must know that I can't abide to see parish clerks. But it don't matter; so long as I know it's the devil, I can put up with it better. I've got some courage in me, only he mustn't come too near me."

"Now I'll ask my wizard," said Little Claus. He trod on the bag and held his ear to it.

"What does he say?"

"He says, 'You can go over there and open the chest that stands in the corner, and you'll see the devil, where he's hiding, but you must hold the lid so that he can't slip out'." "You come and help me hold it," said the farmer, and went over to the chest where his wife had hidden the real parish clerk, who was sitting there in a great fright.

The farmer lifted the lid a little and peeped under it. "Ugh!" he screamed, and jumped back. "Yes, I did see him, and he's for all the world like our clerk. No, now that was a dreadful sight!"

They had to have a drink on the strength of it, and still they sat and drank till late on at night.

"You must sell me that wizard," said the farmer. "Ask what you like for him. Why, I'd give you a whole bushel of money straight off."

"No, I can't do that," said Little Claus; "just think what profit I can make out of that wizard."

17

"Oh dear! I do so want to have him," said the farmer, and kept on begging.

"Well," said Little Claus at last, "as you've been so kind to me giving me a night's lodging, I don't mind. You shall have the wizard for a bushel of money; but I must have a full measure."

"So you shall," said the farmer, "but you must take that chest there away with you. I won't have it an hour longer in the house. Who's to know if he isn't sitting in it still?" Little Claus gave the farmer his sack with the dry hide in it, and got a whole bushel of money, full measure, in exchange. The farmer gave him a big wheelbarrow into the bargain to wheel off his money and the box.

"Good-bye," said Little Claus, and wheeled the barrow off with his money and the big chest in which the clerk was still sitting. On the other side of the forest there was a broad deep river, running so swift that it was hardly possible to swim against the stream. A fine new bridge had been built over it, and Little Claus stopped half-way across it and said, quite loud, so that the clerk in the chest could hear:

"Come, what do I want with this silly chest; it's as heavy as if it was full of stones! I'm quite tired wheeling it. I'll heave it out into the river: if it floats down to me at home, that's all right, and if it doesn't, why, I don't mind." With that he took hold of it with one hand and lifted it a little as if he was going to throw it down into the water.

"No! Stop!" cried the clerk inside the chest. "Do let me get out!"

"O—oh," said Little Claus, pretending to be frightened. "He's in there still. I must get him into the river this minute and drown him." "O no, O no!" cried the clerk. "I'll give you a whole bushel of money if you'll only stop."

"Why, that's a different affair," said Little Claus, and he opened the chest. The clerk crept out quickly and pushed the empty chest over into the river, and went off to his house, where Little Claus got a whole bushel of money. He'd got one already from the farmer, so now he had his wheelbarrow quite full of money.

"Look here, I've got a very fine price for that horse," said he to himself when he got home to his own room and emptied all the money out in a great heap in the middle of the floor. "Big Claus won't like it a bit when he gets to know how rich I've become by the means of my one horse, but I can't tell him right out, all the same."

With that he sent a boy over to Big Claus to borrow a bushel measure.

"Whatever does he want with that?" thought Big Claus, and he smeared some tar on the bottom of it, so that some of what was being measured should stick to it. And so it did, for when he got the measure back there were three new silver groats sticking there.

"What's the meaning of this?" said Big Claus. He ran straight across to the Little one. "Where did you get all that money from?" "Oh, that was for my horse's hide, I sold it yesterday." "Upon my word, that was a good price," said Big Claus. He ran off home, took an axe, knocked all his four horses on the head, got the hides off them, and drove to the town with them. "Hides! Hides! Who'll buy hides?" he went shouting through the streets.

All the shoemakers and tanners came running up and asked what he wanted for them.

"A bushel of money, apiece," said Big Claus.

"Are you mad?" they all said. "Do you think we've got money in bushels?"

"Hides! Hides! Who'll buy hides?" he shouted again, and to everyone who asked what the hides cost, he answered: "A bushel of money!" "He wants to make fools of us," they all said; and then all the shoemakers got out their straps and the tanners their leather aprons and began to thrash Big Claus.

"Hides! Hides!" they sneered at him. "Yes, we'll give you a hide with nice red stripes on it. Out of town with him," they cried, and Big Claus had to make off as quick as ever he could, he'd never been so thrashed in his life. "Very well," said he when he got home, "Little Claus shall be paid out for this. I'll kill him for it."

But now, at Little Claus's house it so happened that his old grandmother had died; true enough she had been very cross and nasty to him, but all the same he was very much grieved, and took the old woman and laid her in his own warm bed to see if she might possibly come to life again. She should lie there all night, and he would sit over in the corner on a stool and sleep there, as he had often done before. And as he sat there in the night the door opened and Big Claus came in with an axe. He knew well enough where Little Claus's bed stood, and went straight to it and hit the dead grandmother's head, thinking it was Little Claus.

"There now," he said, "you won't make a fool of me again!" and off he went home.

"Now that's a real bad man," said Little Claus, "he meant to kill me; it's lucky for old mother that she was dead already, else he'd have had the life out of her." Then he dressed the old grandmother in her Sunday clothes, borrowed a horse of his neighbour, harnessed it to his cart and set the old grandmother up in the back seat so as she couldn't fall out when he drove; and then they rattled off through the forest. When the sun rose they were just by a big inn, and there Little Claus pulled up and went in to get something to eat.

The landlord had ever so much money, and he was a good sort of man, but very hot tempered, as if he was full of pepper and snuff.

"Good morning," said he to Little Claus, "you've got your best clothes on early today."

"Yes," said Little Claus, "I'm off to town with my old grandmother. She's sitting out there in the cart; I can't get her to come indoors. Would you mind taking her a glass of mead? But you must speak to her pretty loud, for she's hard of hearing."

"Yes, that I will," said the landlord, and he poured out a large glass of mead and went out with it to the dead grandmother, who was set up in the cart.

"Here's a glass of mead from your son," said the landlord; but the dead woman didn't say a word: she sat quite still.

"Can't you hear?" shouted the landlord, as loud as he could. "Here's a glass of mead from your son!"

Once more he shouted it out, and once again after that, but

as she didn't stir at all from her seat, he lost his temper and threw the glass straight in her face. The mead ran down her nose and she tumbled over, backwards into the cart, for she was only propped up, and not tied fast.

"Now, now!" shouted Little Claus, rushing out of the inn and seizing hold of the landlord by the collar. "You've been and killed my grandmother! Just look! There's a great hole in her forehead!"

"Oh, dear, what a sad business!" cried the landlord, wringing his hands, "it all comes of me being so hot tempered. My dear friend Little Claus, I'll give you a whole bushel of money and have your grandmother buried as if she was my own, if only you'll hold your tongue; else they'll cut my head off, and that is so unpleasant!"

So Little Claus got a whole bushel of money, and the landlord buried his old grandmother as if she'd been his own.

Now when Little Claus got home again with all the money, he sent his boy over at once to Big Claus to ask if he would kindly lend him a bushel measure. "What's the meaning of this?" said Big Claus. "Haven't I killed him? I must look into this myself." So he went across to Little Claus with the bushel.

"Why, where did you get all that money from?" he asked, and opened his eyes wide when he saw all that had come in.

"It was my grandmother you killed, not me," said Little Claus. "I've just sold her, and got a bushel of money for her."

"My word, that's a good price," said Big Claus; and he hurried off home, took an axe and killed his own old grandmother at once, put her in his cart, drove to town to where the doctor lived, and asked if he wanted to buy a dead person.

"Who is it, and where did you get it from?" asked the doctor. "It's my grandmother," said Big Claus. "I've killed her to get a bushel of money."

"God be good to us," said the doctor, "that's a madman's

talk! For goodness' sake don't say such things. You might lose your head." And then he told him straight out what a fearfully wicked thing it was that he had done, and what a bad man he was, and how he deserved to be punished, and Big Claus got so frightened that he darted out of the doctor's shop and into the cart, whipped up the horses and hurried home. But the doctor and everyone else thought he must be mad, so they let him drive off whither he would.

"You shall be paid out for this," said Big Claus as he drove along the high road. "Yes, you shall be paid out for this, Little Claus." And as soon as ever he got home, he took the biggest sack he could find, went across to Little Claus and said: "Now you've fooled me again! First I killed my horses, and then my old grandmother! It's all your fault, but never again shall you make a fool of me." With that he seized Little Claus by the waist, stuffed him into his sack, threw it over his shoulder and called out to him: "Now I'm off to drown you!"

There was a long bit to go before he came to the river and Little Claus was not over light to carry. The road went close by the church where the organ was playing and the people singing very beautifully. So Big Claus put down his sack with Little Claus in it beside the church door, and thought to himself it might be quite a good thing to go in and listen to a hymn before he went any farther. Little Claus couldn't get away, and everybody was in church; so in he went. "Oh dear! Oh dear!" sighed Little Claus inside the sack. He turned about and about, but he couldn't manage to get the string untied. At that moment there came by an old drover with snow-white hair and a great walking-stick in his hand. Before him was a whole drove of cows and steers, and they ran against the sack where Little Claus was, so that it tumbled over.

"Oh dear!" sighed Little Claus. "I'm quite young, and I've got to go to heaven already!"

"And poor old me," said the drover, "I'm quite old and I can't get there yet!"

"Open the sack," cried Little Claus, "creep in instead of me, and you'll get to heaven straight off!"

"Yes, that I will, and glad to do it," said the drover. He untied the sack for Little Claus, who jumped out at once. "You'll take care of the cattle, won't you?" said the old man, creeping into the sack, which Little Claus tied up, and then went on his way with all the cows and steers.

Soon after, Big Claus came out of the church, loaded the sack on his shoulders again, and thought, rightly enough, it had become quite light, for the old drover weighed not more than half as much as Little Claus. "How light he has become to carry! That's just because I've been and listened to a hymn!" So on he went to the river, which was deep and broad, threw the sack and the old drover out into the water and shouted after him (for of course he thought it was Little Claus): "There now! You shan't make a fool of me any more."

Then he set off home: but when he got to where the roads crossed he met Little Claus coming along with all his cattle. "What's this?" said Big Claus. "Haven't I drowned you?"

"Yes," said Little Claus, "you threw me into the water all right not half an hour ago!"

Little Claus and Big Claus

"But where have you got all those lovely cattle from?" asked Big Claus.

"Why, they're sea cattle," said Little Claus. "I'll tell you the whole story, and very much obliged to you I am for drowning me. I'm on the top now, properly rich I am, I can tell you. I was terribly frightened when I was lying in the sack, and the wind whistled about my ears when you threw me down off the bridge into the cold water. I sank straight to the bottom, but I didn't bump myself, for down there the finest of soft grass grows, and on to that I fell, and the sack came open at once, and the most lovely girl in pure white clothes and with a green wreath on her wet hair, took my hand and said: 'Is that you, Little Claus? Here's some cattle for you to begin with, and four miles farther up the road there's another whole drove waiting, which I'll make you a present of!' Then I made out that the river was a broad highway for the sea people. They were walking along down at the bottom and driving straight up from the sea, right inland to where the river comes to an end. It was so pleasant there with flowers, and the freshest of grass! And the fishes that swam in the water, they darted past my ears like the birds in the air up here. Dear! what fine folk there were, and what a lot of cattle going about along ditches and fences!"

"But why have you come up so quick to us again?" asked Big Claus. "I wouldn't have done that if it was so nice down there." "Why," said Little Claus, "that was just my cleverness! You recollect I told you the sea girl said that four miles along the road (and by the road she meant the river, for she can't get along any other way) there was a whole drove more of cattle for me; but I know how the river goes in bends, first this way and then that way, it's a regular roundabout. No, you can make it shorter by coming up on land if you can, and driving across country to the river again. I shall save almost a couple of miles and get to my sea cattle all the sooner."

"Oh, you are a lucky man!" said Big Claus. "Do you think I should get some sea cattle too if I got down to the bottom of the river?"

"Why, I should think so," said Little Claus. "But I can't carry you to the river in the sack, you're too heavy for me. If you'll walk there yourself and get into the bag, I'll throw you in with the greatest of pleasure."

"I'll be much obliged to you," said Big Claus, "but if I don't get any sea cattle when I get down there, I shall give you a thrashing, depend upon that."

"Oh no, don't be so unkind!" So they went across to the river. When the cattle, which were thirsty, saw the water, they ran as fast as they could to get down there and drink.

"Look what a hurry they're in," said Little Claus, "they're longing to get to the bottom again."

"Yes, but you've got to help me first," said Big Claus, "else you'll get a thrashing!" So he crept into a big sack that had lain on the back of one of the steers. "Just put a stone in it, or I'm afraid I shan't sink," said Big Claus.

"It'll sink all right," said Little Claus; but all the same he put a big stone in the sack, tied the string tight and gave it a push. Splash! There lay Big Claus in the river and sank to the bottom straight.

"I'm *afraid* he won't find those cattle," said Little Claus; and drove off home with what he had.

Pegasus the Winged Horse

————————————————*————————————————

Long ago in the faraway land of Lycea in Asia there lived a fierce monster called the Chimera. It breathed fire and smoke from its huge nostrils and devoured anyone who dared to come near it—sheep, cattle, men, women, children, and even wild beasts. People were afraid to come out of their houses and their King Isobates could neither sleep nor rest for worrying how to rid his land of the evil thing. For what man would be so brave as to undertake so dread a task? The monster had no fewer than three heads, a goat's, a lion's and a serpent's, and from its three mouths there gushed forth long tongues of flame that scorched the countryside and spread destruction far and wide. The Chimera's body was like that of a dragon and its tail like that of a boa constrictor.

At that time a brave and noble young man, Bellerophon by name, chanced to be visiting the King of that land. It was Bellerophon's fondest dream to do some brave and valiant deed, so when the King proposed that he should go out and test his strength against the monster he was only too eager to prepare himself for this mighty task. He told the King that he would either slay the monster or perish in the attempt.

But in his heart of hearts Bellerophon knew he would never be able to slay the monster single-handed. He realized he would simply be burnt to ashes by its fiery breath even before he could get near it. He knew, too, that the only creature that could help him was the wonderful winged horse, Pegasus. But how was he to catch that magical steed, which flew like an eagle over the topmost clouds and which had never yet been tamed by bit or bridle? Pegasus was almost a heavenly creature, coming down to earth only to drink at the fountain of Pirene.

One night as he lay asleep in the moonlight, Bellerophon had a dream in which a woman wearing a golden breastplate and a shining helmet glided towards him. She spoke to Bellerophon and said: "You must wake now and catch the winged horse, Pegasus, when he comes to drink at the fountain." And handing to Bellerophon a finely wrought bridle of gleaming gold, together with a bit, she added: "When you have put this bit between his teeth and the bridle on his head, Pegasus will carry you safely to the Chimera and obey your every command." Bellerophon awoke to find the bridle and bit at his side and he realized that the woman in the dream must have been Athene, the goddess of wisdom, who had been especially sent to help him.

The next day Bellerophon arrived at the fountain of Pirene and hid among the rocks to wait for Pegasus to come. After a long while he heard the swift rush of wings through the clouds and suddenly the dazzling white horse emerged gently and softly and, folding its wings to its flanks, came to land beside the pool. For a time Bellerophon was too dazed with wonder to move and he watched the horse's reflection in the water till he lowered his noble head to drink. In a flash Bellerophon came out from behind the bushes, leapt forward, flung the bridle over Pegasus's head and seated himself on his back. At the same instant Pegasus shot up into the sky with one powerful beat of his wings. It was a most wonderful sight—the beautiful, dazzlingly white animal, with flowing tail and mane, sailing through the air and struggling to throw off his rider. He darted this way and that with such violent speed that Bellerophon could scarcely catch his breath. The horse twisted and turned from cloud to cloud but Bellerophon clung grimly on. Then he plunged upwards, climbing higher and higher into the clouds, turning wild somersaults and beating his wings in a frenzy of terror, then suddenly swooped down again, but Bellerophon sat ever firm and now felt able to fit the enchanted bit between Pegasus's teeth. No sooner was this done than the horse, as if by magic, grew calm and yielding to his rider's touch. Bellerophon gently stroked the enchanted steed and said softly but urgently: "I need your help, Pegasus; without it I cannot slay the dread Chimera and rid the fair land of Lycea of its fearful scourge."

Pegasus now began to fly ever more gently until he came down to a halt near the fountain. But when Bellerophon, still holding the bridle, leapt from his back to look into the horse's eyes, he saw they were filled with tears and his brave heart melted. He felt he had trapped this wonderful wild creature of the air and robbed him of his liberty. He removed the bridle and said, "Pegasus, I have no right to take away your freedom to roam the skies and fly unbridled among the clouds." At these words Pegasus soared upward and was soon only a speck over the mountain peaks and Bellerophon turned sadly away. Yet somehow he was glad that he had given the steed his freedom. Then suddenly, to his indescribable joy, he felt a rush of wind behind him and Pegasus's head pushing under his arm. And now Bellerophon knew for certain that Pegasus had come back of his own free will to help him in his great task.

From now on Pegasus was obedient to every whisper and touch of his rider. Man and horse began to practise as though they were fighting a real enemy. They galloped through the air, making sudden twists and leaps, now darting up, now plunging down, and now remaining perfectly still above the clouds. This went on for several days, until Bellerophon and Pegasus felt they had known one another all their lives.

Then when the day came for Bellerophon to meet the Chimera, he took his shining sword and shield and leapt on to Pegasus's back and flew away over seas and deserts, mountains and valleys, rocks and chasms, until they arrived at a deserted cave where nothing could be seen but heaps of rotting bones. This was the monster's lair. Bellerophon stroked his horse's mane and whispered in his ear: "Dear Pegasus, I will not ask you to come any farther. I do not want your beautiful body to be maimed by the monster's breath. Let me fight the Chimera alone, on foot." Pegasus, in reply, nuzzled his head against Bellerophon's arm.

Encouraged by this, Bellerophon gripped his sword firmly and galloped towards the entrance of the cave. They were met by the most fearsome roars and blinded by the black smoke and flames belching out from the mouth of the Chimera's cave. The stench of the sulphurous fumes caused the horse to shy away with a snort and Bellerophon sneezed violently and covered his eyes. But only for a moment, for when he removed his hand from his eyes his magic steed was swooping down like a swift ray of light to where the monster's three heads lay writhing and snarling, looking indeed like three separate, hideous monsters. Skilfully wheeling Pegasus away, he smote at one of the heads as it belched forth its fiery flames. He looked down and saw that he had severed the goat's head, which now lay bleeding in the dust. The monster roared with ever greater fury and sprang up towards the rider and his horse with its ugly claws extended and its serpent's tail lashing madly about it. The nimble Pegasus was not to be caught. Quick as lightning he was up aloft and then swooped down again, allowing Bellerophon to make a mighty cut at the lion's head, which, in its turn, then lay gory and life-less beside the goat's. The Chimera's remaining head, the head of the venomous, hissing serpent, writhed and spluttered in raging fury and it stood up on its tail in an effort to ensnare its nimble adversaries. Mustering every ounce of strength, Bellero-phon drove his steed straight at it for the last time. The monster's shrieks and snarlings were terrible to hear and, many miles away, King Isobates and his people trembled at the sound. This time, however, the monster flung itself at its enemies, clinging to the horse's flanks as he soared upward into the clouds. Bellero-phon felt the serpent's tail winding around his waist, felt the scorching flames sear his face and saw the serpent's gaping jaws ready to devour him. He protected himself with his shield and with a powerful thrust plunged his sword deep inside the ser-pent's maw until it reached down to its very heart. With a deafening shriek and relaxing its powerful tail from around

Bellerophon's body, the monster (or what remained of it) went hurtling to its lair far, far below. And as it fell it was devoured by its own flames.

Pegasus soared gracefully upward into the heavens and Bellerophon gave one last look at the dread scene. Then the noble steed flew downward towards the earth and when they landed the rider embraced his gallant mount and tended his wounds.

And thus, thanks to Pegasus and Bellerophon, was the fair land of Lycea freed at last from the dread scourge of the Chimera.

Melisande or Long and Short Division

---*---

When the Princess Melisande was born, her mother, the Queen, wished to have a christening party, but the King put his foot down and said he would not have it.

"I've seen too much trouble come of christening parties," said he. "However carefully you keep your visiting-book, some fairy or other is sure to get left out, and you know what that leads to. Why, even in my own family, the most shocking things have occurred. The Fairy Malevola was not asked to my great-grandmother's christening—and you know all about the spindle and the hundred years' sleep."

"Perhaps you're right," said the Queen. "My own cousin by marriage forgot some stuffy old fairy or other when she was sending out the cards for her daughter's christening, and the old wretch turned up at the last moment, and the girl drops toads out of her mouth to this day."

"Just so. And there was that business of the mouse and the kitchen-maids," said the King; "we'll have no nonsense about it. I'll be her godfather, and you shall be her godmother, and we won't ask a single fairy; then none of them can be offended."

"Unless they all are," said the Queen.

And that was exactly what happened. When the King and

Queen and the baby got back from the christening the parlour-maid met them at the door, and said:

"Please, Your Majesty, several ladies have called. I told them you were not at home, but they all said they'd wait."

"Are they in the parlour?" asked the Queen.

"I've shown them into the Throne Room, Your Majesty," said the parlourmaid. "You see there are several of them."

There were about seven hundred. The great Throne Room was crammed with fairies, of all ages and of all degrees of beauty and ugliness—good fairies and bad fairies, flower fairies and moon fairies, fairies like spiders and fairies like butterflies—and as the Queen opened the door and began to say how sorry she was to have kept them waiting, they all cried, with one voice: "Why didn't you ask me to your christening party?"

"I haven't had a party," said the Queen, and she turned to the King and whispered, "I told you so." This was her only consolation.

"You've had a christening," said the fairies, all together.

"I'm very sorry," said the poor Queen, but Malevola pushed forward and said, "Hold your tongue!" most rudely.

Malevola is the oldest, as well as the most wicked, of the fairies. She is deservedly unpopular, and has been left out of more christening parties than all the rest of the fairies put together.

."Don't begin to make excuses," she said, shaking her finger at the Queen. "That only makes your conduct worse. You know well enough what happens if a fairy is left out of a christening party. We are all going to give our christening presents now. As the fairy of highest social position, I shall begin. The Princess shall be bald."

The Queen nearly fainted as Malevola drew back, and another fairy, in a smart bonnet with snakes in it, stepped forward with a rustle of bats' wings. But the King stepped forward too.

"No, you don't!" said he. "I wonder at you, ladies, I do indeed. How can you be so unfairylike? Have none of you been to school—have none of you studied the history of your own race? Surely you don't need a poor, ignorant King like me to tell you that this is no go?"

"How dare you?" cried the fairy in the bonnet, and the snakes in it quivered as she tossed her head. "It is my turn, and I say the Princess shall be——"

The King actually put his hand over her mouth.

"Look here," he said; "I won't have it. Listen to reason—or you'll be sorry afterwards. A fairy who breaks the traditions of fairy history goes out—you know she does—like the flame of a candle. And all the tradition shows that only one bad fairy is ever forgotten at a christening party and the good ones are always invited; so either this is not a christening party, or else you were all invited except one, and, by her own showing, that was Malevola. It nearly always is. Do I make myself clear?"

Several of the better-class fairies who had been led away by Malevola's influence murmured that there was something in what His Majesty said.

"Try it, if you don't believe me," said the King; "give your nasty gifts to my innocent child—but as sure as you do, out you go, like a candle-flame. Now, then, will you risk it?"

No one answered, and presently several fairies came up to the Queen, and said what a pleasant party it had been, but they really must be going. This example decided the rest. One by one all the fairies said good-bye and thanked the Queen for the delightful afternoon they had spent with her.

"It's been quite too lovely," said the lady with the snake-bonnet; "do ask us again soon, dear Queen. I shall be so longing to see you again, and the dear baby," and off she went, with the snake-trimming quivering more than ever.

When the very last fairy was gone the Queen ran to look at

the baby—she tore off its Honiton lace cap and burst into tears. For all the baby's downy golden hair came off with the cap, and the Princess Melisande was as bald as an egg.

"Don't cry, my love," said the King. "I have a wish lying by, which I've never had occasion to use. My fairy godmother gave it me for a wedding present, but since then I've had nothing to wish for!"

"Thank you, dear," said the Queen, smiling through her tears.

"I'll keep the wish till baby grows up," the King went on. "And then I'll give it to her, and if she likes to wish for hair she can."

"Oh, won't you wish for it now?" said the Queen dropping mixed tears and kisses on the baby's round, smooth head.

"No, dearest. She may want something else more when she grows up. And besides, her hair may grow by itself."

But it never did. Princess Melisande grew up as beautiful as the sun and as good as gold, but never a hair grew on that little head of hers. The Queen sewed her little caps of green silk, and the Princess's pink and white face looked out of these like a flower peeping out of its bud. And every day as she grew older she grew dearer, and as she grew dearer she grew better, and as she grew more good she grew more beautiful.

Now, when she was grown up the Queen said to the King:

"My love, our dear daughter is old enough to know what she wants. Let her have the wish."

So the King wrote to his fairy godmother and sent the letter by a butterfly. He asked if he might hand on to his daughter the wish the fairy had given him for a wedding present.

"I have never had occasion to use it," said he, "though it has always made me happy to remember that I had such a thing in the house. The wish is as good as new, and my daughter is now of an age to appreciate so valuable a present."

Melisande or Long and Short Division

To which the fairy replied by return of butterfly:

Dear King,

Pray do whatever you like with my poor little present. I had quite forgotten it, but I am pleased to think that you have treasured my humble keepsake all these years.

Your affectionate godmother,
FORTUNA F.

So the King unlocked his gold safe with the several diamond-handled keys that hung at his girdle, and took out the wish and gave it to his daughter.

And Melisande said: "Father, I will wish all your subjects should be quite happy."

But they were that already, because the King and Queen were so good. So the wish did not go off.

So then she said: "Then I wish them all to be good."

But they were that already, because they were happy. So again the wish hung fire.

Then the Queen said: "Dearest, for my sake, wish what I tell you."

"Why, of course I will," said Melisande. The Queen whispered in her ear, and Melisande nodded. Then she said, aloud:

"I wish I had golden hair a yard long, and that it would grow an inch every day, and grow twice as fast every time it was cut, and——"

"Stop," cried the King. And the wish went off, and the next moment the Princess stood smiling at him through a shower of golden hair.

"Oh, how lovely," said the Queen. "What a pity you interrupted her, dear; she hadn't finished."

"What was the end?" asked the King.

"Oh," said Melisande, "I was only going to say, 'and twice as thick'."

Melisande or Long and Short Division

"It's a very good thing you didn't," said the King. "You've done about enough." For he had a mathematical mind, and could do the sums about the grains of wheat on the chess-board, and the nails in the horse's shoes, in his royal head without any trouble at all.

"Why, what's the matter?" asked the Queen.

"You'll know soon enough," said the King. "Come, let's be happy while we may. Give me a kiss, little Melisande, and then go to nurse and ask her to teach you how to comb your hair."

"I know," said Melisande, "I've often combed mother's."

"Your mother has beautiful hair," said the King; "but I fancy you will find your own less easy to manage."

And, indeed, it was so. The Princess's hair began by being a yard long, and it grew an inch every night. If you know anything at all about the simplest sums you will see that in about five weeks her hair was about two yards long. This is a very inconvenient length. It trails on the floor, and sweeps up all the dust, and though in palaces, of course, it is all gold-dust, still it is not nice to have it in your hair. And the Princess's hair was growing an inch every night. When it was three yards long, the Princess could not bear it any longer—it was so heavy and so hot—so she borrowed nurse's cutting-out scissors and cut it all off, and then for a few hours she was comfortable. But the hair went on growing, and now it grew twice as fast as before; so that in·thirty-six days it was as long as ever. The poor Princess cried with tiredness; when she couldn't bear it any more she cut her hair and was comfortable for a very little time. For the hair now grew four times as fast as at first, and in eighteen days it was as long as before, and she had to have it cut. Then it grew eight inches a day, and the next time it was cut it grew sixteen inches a day, and then thirty-two inches and sixty-four and a hundred and twenty-eight inches a day, and so on, growing twice as fast after each cutting, till the Princess would go to bed at night with

her hair clipped short, and wake up in the morning with yards and yards and yards of golden hair flowing all about the room, so that she could not move without pulling her own hair, and nurse had to come and cut the hair off before she could get out of bed.

"I wish I was bald again," sighed poor Melisande, looking at the little green caps she used to wear, and she cried herself to sleep o' nights between the golden billows of the golden hair. But she never let her mother see her cry, because it was the Queen's fault, and Melisande did not want to seem to reproach her.

When first the Princess's hair grew her mother sent locks of it to all her royal relations, who had them set in rings and brooches. Later the Queen was able to send enough for bracelets and girdles. But presently so much hair was cut off that they had to burn it. Then when autumn came all the crops failed; it seemed as though all the gold of harvest had gone into the Princess's hair. And there was a famine. Then Melisande said:

"It seems a pity to waste all my hair; it does grow so very fast. Couldn't we stuff things with it, or something, and sell them, to feed the people?"

So the King called a council of merchants, and they sent out samples of the Princess's hair, and soon orders came pouring in; and the Princess's hair became the staple export of that country. They stuffed pillows with it, and they stuffed beds with it. They made ropes of it for sailors to use, and curtains for hanging in kings' palaces. They made hair-cloth of it, for hermits, and other people who wished to be uncomfy. But it was so soft and silky that it only made them happy and warm, which they did not wish to be. So the hermits gave up wearing it, and, instead, mothers bought it for their little babies, and all well-born infants wore little shirts of Princess hair-cloth.

And still the hair grew and grew. And the people were fed and the famine came to an end.

Then the King said: "It was all very well while the famine lasted—but now I shall write to my fairy godmother and see if something cannot be done."

So he wrote and sent the letter by a skylark, and by return of bird came this answer:

"Why not advertise for a competent prince? Offer the usual reward."

So the King sent out his heralds all over the world to proclaim that any respectable prince with proper referencse should marry the Princess Melisande if he could stop her hair growing.

Then from far and near came trains of princes anxious to try their luck, and they brought all sorts of nasty things with them in bottles and round wooden boxes. The Princess tried all the remedies, but she did not like any of the princes, so in her heart she was rather glad that none of the nasty things in bottles and boxes made the least difference to her hair.

The Princess had to sleep in the great Throne Room now, because no other room was big enough to hold her and her hair. When she woke in the morning the long room would be quite full of her golden hair, packed tight and thick like wool in a barn. And every night when she had had the hair cut close to her head she would sit in her green silk gown by the window and cry, and kiss the little green caps she used to wear, and wish herself bald again.

It was as she sat crying there on Midsummer Eve that she first saw Prince Florizel.

He had come to the palace that evening, but he would not appear in her presence with the dust of travel on him, and she had retired with her hair borne by twenty pages before he had bathed and changed his garments and entered the reception-room.

Now he was walking in the garden in the moonlight, and he looked up and she looked down, and for the first time Melisande, looking on a prince, wished that he might have the power to stop her hair from growing. As for the Prince, he wished many things, and the first was granted him. For he said:

"You are Melisande?"

"And you are Florizel?"

"There are many roses round your window," said he to her, "and none down here."

She threw him one of three white roses she held in her hand. Then he said:

"White rose-trees are strong. May I climb up to you?"

"Surely," said the Princess.

So he climbed up to the window.

"Now," said he, "if I can do what your father asks, will you marry me?"

42

Melisande or Long and Short Division

"My father has promised that I shall," said Melisande, playing with the white roses in her hand.

"Dear Princess," said he, "your father's promise is nothing to me. I want yours. Will you give it to me?"

"Yes," said she, and gave him the second rose.

"I want your hand."

"Yes," she said.

"And your heart with it."

"Yes," said the Princess, and she gave him the third rose.

"And a kiss to seal the promise."

"Yes," said she.

"And a kiss to go with the hand."

"Yes," she said.

"And a kiss to bring the heart."

"Yes," said the Princess, and she gave him the three kisses.

"Now," said he, when he had given them back to her, "to-night do not go to bed. Stay by your window, and I will stay down here in the garden and watch. And when your hair has grown to the filling of your room call to me, and then do as I tell you."

"I will," said the Princess.

So at dewy sunrise the Prince, lying on the turf beside the sun-dial, heard her voice:

"Florizel! Florizel! My hair has grown so long that it is pushing me out of the window."

"Get out on to the window-sill," said he, "and twist your hair three times round the great iron hook that is there."

And she did.

Then the Prince climbed up the rose bush with his naked sword in his teeth, and he took the Princess's hair in his hand about a yard from her head and said:

"Jump!"

The Princess jumped, and screamed, for there she was hanging from the hook by a yard and a half of her bright hair; the Prince tightened his grasp of the hair and drew his sword across it.

Then he let her down gently by her hair till her feet were on the grass, and jumped down after her.

They stayed talking in the garden till all the shadows had crept under their proper trees and the sun-dial said it was breakfast-time.

Then they went into breakfast, and all the Court crowded round to wonder and admire. For the Princess's hair had not grown.

"How did you do it?" asked the King, shaking Florizel warmly by the hand.

"The simplest thing in the world," said Florizel modestly. "You have always cut the hair off the Princess. I just cut the Princess off the hair."

"Humph!" said the King, who had a logical mind. And during breakfast he more than once looked anxiously at his daughter. When they got up from breakfast the Princess rose with the rest, but she rose and rose and rose, till it seemed as though there would never be an end of it. The Princess was nine feet high.

"I feared as much," said the King sadly. "I wonder what will be the rate of progression. You see," he said to poor Florizel, "when we cut the hair off it grows—when we cut the Princess off she grows. I wish you had happened to think of that!"

The Princess went on growing. By dinner-time she was so large that she had to have her dinner brought out into the garden because she was too large to get indoors. But she was too unhappy to be able to eat anything. And she cried so much that there was quite a pool in the garden, and several pages were nearly drowned. So she remembered her Alice in Wonderland, and stopped crying at once. But she did not stop growing. She grew bigger and bigger and bigger, till she had to go outside the palace gardens and sit on the common, and even that was too small to hold her comfortably, for every hour she grew twice as much as she had done the hour before. And nobody knew what to do, nor where the Princess was to sleep. Fortunately her clothes had grown with her, or she would have been very cold indeed, and now she sat on the common in her green gown, embroidered with gold, looking like a great hill covered with gorse in flower.

You cannot possibly imagine how large the Princess was growing, and her mother stood wringing her hands on the castle tower, and the Prince Florizel looked on broken-hearted to see his Princess snatched from his arms and turned into a lady as big as a mountain.

The King did not weep or look on. He sat down at once and wrote to his fairy godmother, asking her advice. He sent a weasel with the letter, and by return of weasel he got his own letter back again, marked, "Gone away. Left no address."

It was now, when the kingdom was plunged into gloom, that a neighbouring King took it into his head to send an invading army against the island where Melisande lived. They came in ships and they landed in great numbers, and Melisande, looking down from her height, saw alien soldiers marching on the sacred soil of her country.

"I don't mind so much now," said she, "if I can really be of some use this size."

And she picked up the army of the enemy in handfuls and double-handfuls, and put them back in their ships, and gave a little flip to each transport ship with her finger and thumb, which sent the ships off so fast that they never stopped till they reached their own country, and when they arrived there the whole army to a man said it would rather be court-martialled a hundred times than go near the palace again.

Melisande or Long and Short Division

Meanwhile Melisande, sitting in the highest hill on the island, felt the land trembling and shivering under her giant feet.

"I do believe I'm getting too heavy," she said, and jumped off the island into the sea, which was just up to her ankles. Just then a great fleet of warships and gunboats and torpedo boats came ni sight, on their way to attack the island.

Melisande could easily have sunk them all with one kick, but she did not like to do this because it might have drowned the sailors, and besides, it might have swamped the island.

So she simply stooped and picked the island as you would pick a mushroom—for, of course, all islands are supported by a stalk underneath—and carried it away to another part of the world. So that when the warships got to where the island was marked on the map they found nothing but sea, and a very rough sea it was, because the Princess had churned it all up with her ankles as she walked away through it with the island.

When Melisande reached a suitable place, very sunny and warm, and with no sharks in the water, she set down the island; and the people made it fast with anchors, and then everyone went to bed, thanking the kind fate which had sent them so great a Princess to help them in their need, and calling her the saviour of her country and the bulwark of the nation.

But it is poor work being the nation's bulwark and your country's saviour when you are miles high, and have no one to talk to, and when all you want is to be your humble right size again and to marry your sweetheart. And when it was dark the Princess came close to the island, and looked down, from far up, at her palace and her tower, and cried and cried and cried. It does not matter how much you cry into the sea, it hardly makes any difference, however large you may be. Then when everything was quite dark the Princess looked up at the stars.

"I wonder how soon I shall be big enough to knock my head against them," she said.

And she stood star-gazing and she heard a whisper right in her ear. A very little whisper, but quite plain.

"Cut off your hair!" it said.

Now, everything the Princess was wearing had grown big along with her, so that now there dangled from her golden girdle a pair of scissors as big as the Malay Peninsula, together with a pincushion the size of the Isle of Wight, and a yard measure that would have gone round Australia.

And when she heard the little, little voice, she knew it, small as it was, for the dear voice of Prince Florizel, and she whipped out the scissors from her gold case and snip, snip, snipped all her hair off, and it fell into the sea. The coral insects got hold of it at once and set to work on it, and now they have made it into the biggest coral reef in the world; but that has nothing to do with the story.

Then the voice said, "Get close to the island," and the Princess did, but she could not get very close because she was so large, and she looked up again at the stars and they seemed to be much farther off.

Then the voice said, "Be ready to swim," and she felt something climb out of her ear and clamber down her arm. The stars got farther and farther away, and next moment the Princess found herself swimming in the sea, and Prince Florizel swimming beside her.

"I crept on to your hand when you were carrying the island," he explained, when their feet touched the sand and they walked in through the shallow water, "and I got into your ear with an ear-trumpet. You never noticed me because you were so great then."

"Oh, my dear Prince," cried Melisande, falling into his arms, "you have saved me. I am my proper size again."

So they went home and told the King and Queen. Both were very very happy, but the King rubbed his chin with his hand and said:

Melisande or Long and Short Division

"You've certainly had some fun for your money, young man, but don't you see that we're just where we were before? Why, the child's hair is growing already."

And indeed it was.

Then once more the King sent a letter to his godmother. He sent it by a flying-fish, and by return of fish came the answer:

"Just back from my holidays. Sorry for your troubles. Why not try scales?"

And on this message the whole court pondered for weeks.

But the Prince caused a pair of gold scales to be made, and hung them up in the palace gardens under a big oak-tree. And one morning he said to the Princess:

"My darling Melisande, I must really speak seriously to you. We are getting on in life. I am nearly twenty: it is time that we thought of being settled. Will you trust me entirely and get into one of those gold scales?"

So he took her down into the garden, and helped her into the scale, and she curled up in it in her green and gold gown, like a little grass mound with buttercups on it.

"And what is going into the other scale?" asked Melisande.

"Your hair," said Florizel. "You see, when your hair is cut off it grows, and when you are cut off your hair you grow—oh my heart's delight, I can never forget how you grew, never! But if, when your hair is no more than you, and you are no more than your hair, I snip the scissors between you and it, then neither you nor your hair can possibly decide which ought to go on growing."

"Suppose both did," said the poor Princess humbly.

"Impossible," said the Prince, with a shudder; "there are limits even to Malevola's malevolence. And, besides, Fortuna said, 'Scales.' Will you try it?"

"I will do whatever you wish," said the poor Princess, "but let me kiss my father and mother once, and Nurse, and you too, my dear, in case I grow large again and can kiss nobody any more."

So they came one by one and kissed the Princess.

Then the nurse cut off the Princess's hair, and at once it began to grow at a frightful rate.

The King and Queen and nurse busily packed it, as it grew, into the other scale, and gradually the scale went down a little. The Prince stood waiting between the scales with his drawn sword, and just before the two were equal he struck. But during the time his sword took to flash through the air the Princess's hair grew a yard or two, so that at the instant when he struck the balance was true.

"You are a young man of sound judgement," said the King, embracing him, while the Queen and the nurse ran to help the Princess out of the gold scale.

The scale full of golden hair bumped down on to the ground as the Princess stepped out of the other one, and stood there before those who loved her, laughing and crying with happiness, because she remained her proper size, and her hair was not growing any more.

She kissed the Prince a hundred times, and the very next day they were married. Everyone remarked on the beauty of the bride, and it was noticed that her hair was quite short—only five feet five and a quarter inches long—just down to her pretty ankles. Because the scales had been ten feet ten and a half inches apart, and the Prince, having a straight eye, had cut the golden hair exactly in the middle!

A Chinese Fairy Tale

———————————*———————————

Tiki-Pu was a small grub of a thing; but he had a true love of Art deep down in his soul. There it hung mewing and complaining, struggling to work its way out through the raw exterior that bound it.

Tiki-Pu's master professed to be an artist: he had apprentices and students, who came daily to work under him, and a large studio littered about with the performances of himself and his pupils. On the walls hung also a few real works by the older men, all long since dead.

This studio Tiki-Pu swept; for those who worked in it he ground colours, washed brushes, and ran errands, bringing them their dog chops and bird's nest soup from the nearest eating-house whenever they were too busy to go out for it themselves. He himself had to feed mainly on the breadcrumbs which the students screwed into pellets for their drawings and then threw about on the floor. It was on the floor, also, that he had to sleep at night.

Tiki-Pu looked after the blinds, and mended the window-panes, which were often broken when the apprentices threw their brushes and mahl-sticks at him. Also he strained rice-paper over the linen-stretchers, ready for the painters to work on; and for a treat, now and then, a lazy one would allow him to mix a colour for him. Then it was that Tiki-Pu's soul came down into

51

his finger-tips, and his heart beat so that he gasped for joy. Oh, the yellow and the greens, and the lakes and cobalts, and the purples which sprang from the blending of them! Sometimes it was all he could do to keep himself from crying out.

Tiki-Pu, while he squatted and ground at the colour-powders, would listen to his master lecturing to the students. He knew by heart the names of all the painters and their schools, and the

name of the great leader of them all who had lived and passed from their midst more than three hundred years ago; he knew that too, a name like the sound of the wind, Wio-Wani: the big picture at the end of the studio was by him.

That picture! To Tiki-Pu it seemed worth all the rest of the world put together. He knew, too, the story which was told of it, making it as holy to his eyes as the tombs of his own ancestors. The apprentices joked over it, calling it "Wio-Wani's back-door", "Wio-Wani's night-cap", and many other nicknames; but Tiki-Pu was quite sure, since the picture was so beautiful, that the story must be true.

Wio-Wani, at the end of a long life, had painted it; a garden full of trees and sunlight, with high-standing flowers and green paths, and in their midst a palace. "The place where I would like to rest," said Wio-Wani, when it was finished.

So beautiful was it then, that the Emperor himself had come to see it; and gazing enviously at those peaceful walks, and the palace nestling among the trees, had sighed and owned that he too would be glad of such a resting-place. Then Wio-Wani stepped into the picture, and walked away along a path till he came, looking quite small and far-off, to a low door in the palace-wall. Opening it, he turned and beckoned to the Emperor; but the Emperor did not follow; so Wio-Wani went in by himself, and shut the door between himself and the world for ever.

That happened three hundred years ago; but for Tiki-Pu the story was as fresh and true as if it had happened yesterday. When he was left to himself in the studio, all alone and locked up for the night, Tiki-Pu used to go and stare at the picture till it was too dark to see, and at the little palace with the door in its wall by which Wio-Wani had disappeared out of life. Then his soul would go down into his finger-tips, and he would knock softly and fearfully at the beautifully painted door, saying, "Wio-Wani, are you there?"

Little by little in the long-thinking nights, and the slow early mornings when light began to creep back through the papered windows of the studio, Tiki-Pu's soul became too much for him. He who could strain paper, and grind colours, and wash brushes, had everything within reach for becoming an artist, if it was the will of Fate that he should be one.

He began timidly at first, but in a little while he grew bold. With the first wash of light he was up from his couch on the hard floor and was daubing his soul out on scraps, and odds and ends, and stolen pieces of rice-paper.

Before long the short spell of daylight which lay between dawn and the arrival of the apprentices to their work did not suffice him. It took him so long to hide all traces of his doings, to wash out the brushes, and rinse clean the paint-pots he had used, and on the top of that to get the studio swept and dusted, that there was hardly time left him in which to indulge the itching of his fingers.

Driven by necessity, he became a pilferer of candle-ends, picking them from their sockets in the lanterns which the students carried on dark nights. Now and then one of these would remember that, when last used, his lantern had had a candle in it, and would accuse Tiki-Pu of having stolen it. "It is true," he would confess, "I was hungry—I have eaten it." The lie was so probable, he was believed easily, and was well beaten accordingly. Down in the ragged linings of his coat Tiki-Pu could hear the candle-ends rattling as the buffeting and chastisement fell upon him, and often he trembled lest his hoard should be discovered. But the truth of the matter never leaked out; and at night, as soon as he guessed that all the world outside was in bed, Tiki-Pu would mount one of his candles on a wooden stand and paint by the light of it, blinding himself over the task, till the dawn came and gave him a better and cheaper light to work by.

Tiki-Pu quite hugged himself over the results; he believed he was doing very well. "If only Wio-Wani were here to teach me," thought he, "I would be in the way to becoming a great painter!"

The resolution came to him one night that Wio-Wani should teach him. So he took a large piece of rice-paper and strained it, and sitting down opposite "Wio-Wani's back door", began painting. He had never set himself so big a task as this; by the dim stumbling light of his candle he strained his eyes nearly blind over the difficulties of it; and at last was almost driven to despair. How the trees stood row behind row, with air and sunlight between, and how the path went in and out, winding its way up to the little door in the palace-wall, were mysteries he could not fathom. He peered and peered and dropped tears into his paint-pots; but the secret of the mystery of such painting was far beyond him.

The door in the palace-wall opened; out came a little old man and began walking down the pathway towards him.

The soul of Tiki-Pu gave a sharp leap in his grubby little body. "That must be Wio-Wani himself and no other!" cried his soul.

Tiki-Pu pulled off his cap and threw himself down on the floor with reverent grovellings. When he dared to look up again Wio-Wani stood over him big and fine; just within the edge of the canvas he stood and reached out a hand.

"Come along with me, Tiki-Pu!" said the great one. "If you want to know how to paint I will teach you."

"Oh, Wio-Wani, were you there all the while?" cried Tiki-Pu ecstatically, leaping up and clutching with his smeary little puds the hand which the old man extended to him.

"I was there," said Wio-Wani, "looking at you out of my little window. Come along in!"

Tiki-Pu took a heave and swung himself into the picture, and fairly capered when he found his feet among the flowers of Wio-Wani's beautiful garden. Wio-Wani had turned, and was ambling gently back to the door of his palace, beckoning to the small one to follow him; and there stood Tiki-Pu opening his mouth like a fish to all the wonders that surrounded him. "Celestiality, may I speak?" he said suddenly.

"Speak," replied Wio-Wani; "what is it?"

"The Emperor, was he not the very flower of fools not to follow when you told him?"

"I cannot say," answered Wio Wani, "but he certainly was no artist."

Then he opened the door, that door which he had so beautifully painted, and led Tiki-Pu in. Outside the little candle-end sat and guttered by itself, till the wick fell overboard, and the flame kicked itself out, leaving the studio in darkness and solitude to wait for the growings of another dawn.

It was full day before Tiki reappeared; he came running down the green path in great haste, jumped out of the frame on to the studio floor, and began tidying up his own messes of the night and the apprentices of the previous day. Only just in time did he have things ready by the hour when his master and the others returned to their work.

All that day they kept scratching their left ears, and could not think why; but Tiki-Pu knew, for he was saying over to himself all the things that Wio-Wani, the great painter, had been saying about them and their precious productions. And as he ground their colours for them and washed their brushes, and filled his famished little body with the breadcrumbs they threw away, little they guessed from what an immeasurable distance he looked down upon them all, and had Wio-Wani's word for it tickling his right ear all the day long.

Now before long Tiki-Pu's master noticed a change in him; and though he bullied him, and thrashed him, and did all that a careful master should do, he could not get the change out of him. So in a short while he grew suspicious. "What is the boy up to?" he wondered. "I have my eye on him all day: it must be at night that he gets into mischief."

It did not take Tiki-Pu's master a night's watching to find that something surreptitious was certainly going on. When it was dark he took up his post outside the studio, to see whether by any chance Tiki-Pu had some way of getting out; and before long he saw a faint light showing through the window. So he came and thrust his finger softly through one of the panes, and put his eye to the hole.

There inside was a candle burning on a stand, and Tiki-Pu squatting with paint-pots and brush in front of Wio-Wani's last masterpiece.

"What fine piece of burglary is this?" thought he; "what serpent have I been harbouring in my bosom? Is this beast of a grub of a boy thinking to make himself a painter and cut me out of my reputation and prosperity?" For even at that distance he could plainly perceive that the work of this boy went head and shoulders beyond his, or that of any painter living.

Presently Wio-Wani opened his door and came down the path, as was his habit now each night, to call Tiki-Pu to his lesson. He advanced to the front of the picture and beckoned for Tiki-Pu to come in with him; and Tiki-Pu's master grew clammy at the knees as he beheld Tiki-Pu catch hold of Wio-Wani's hand and jump into the picture, and skip up the green path by Wio-Wani's side, and in through the little door that Wio-Wani had painted so beautifully in the end wall of his palace!

For a time Tiki-Pu's master stood glued to the spot with grief and horror. "Oh, you deadly little underling! Oh, you poisonous little caretaker, you parasite, you vampire, you fly in amber!" cried he, "is that where you get your training? Is it there that you dare to go trespassing; into a picture that I purchased for my own pleasure and profit, and not at all for yours? Very soon we will see whom it really belongs to!"

He ripped out the paper of the largest window-pane and pushed his way through into the studio. Then in great haste he took up paint-pot and brush, and sacrilegiously set himself to work upon Wio-Wani's last masterpiece. In the place of the doorway by which Tiki-Pu had entered he painted a solid brick wall; twice over he painted it, making it two bricks thick; brick

58

by brick he painted it, and mortared every brick to its place. And when he had quite finished, he laughed, and called, "Good night, Tiki-Pu!" and went home to be quite happy.

The next day all the apprentices were wondering what had become of Tiki-Pu; but as the master himself said nothing, and as another boy came to act as colour-grinder and brush-washer to the establishment, they very soon forgot all about him.

In the studio the master used to sit at work with his students all about him, and a mind full of ease and contentment. Now and then he would throw a glance across to the bricked-up door-way of Wio-Wani's palace, and laugh to himself, thinking how well he had served out Tiki-Pu for his treachery and presumption.

One day—it was five years after the disappearance of Tiku-Pu—he was giving his apprentices a lecture on the glories and the beauties and the wonders of Wio-Wani's painting—how nothing for colour could excel, or for mystery could equal it. To add point to his eloquence, he stood waving his hands before Wio-Wani's last masterpiece, and all his students and apprentices sat round him and looked.

Suddenly he stopped at mid-word, and broke off in the full flight of his eloquence, as he saw something like a hand come and take down the top brick from the face of paint which he had laid over the little door in the palace-wall which Wio-Wani had so beautifully painted. In another moment there was no doubt about it; brick by brick the wall was being pulled down, in spite of its double thickness.

The lecturer was altogether too dumbfounded and terrified to utter a word. He and all his apprentices stood round and stared while the demolition of the wall proceeded. Before long he recognized Wio-Wani with his flowing white beard; it was his handiwork this pulling down of the wall! He still had a brick in his hand when he stepped through the opening that he had made, and close after him stepped Tiki-Pu!

Tiki-Pu had grown tall and strong—he was even handsome; but for all that his old master recognized him, and saw with an envious foreboding that under his arms he carried many rolls and stretchers and portfolios, and other belongings of his craft. Clearly Tiki-Pu was coming back into the world, and was going to be a great painter.

Down the garden path came Wio-Wani, and Tiki-Pu walked after him; Tiki-Pu was so tall that his head stood well over Wio-Wani's shoulders—old man and young man together made a handsome pair.

How big Wio-Wani grew as he walked down the avenue of his garden and into the foreground of his picture! and how big the brick in his hand! and ah, how angry he seemed!

Wio-Wani came right down to the edge of the picture-frame and held up the brick. "What did you do that for?" he asked.

"I . . . didn't!" Tiki-Pu's old master was beginning to reply; and the lie was still rolling on his tongue when the weight of the brick-bat, which he himself had reared, became his own tombstone.

Just inside the picture-frame stood Tiki-Pu, kissing the wonderful hands of Wio-Wani, which had taught him all their skill. "Good-bye, Tiki-Pu!" said Wio-Wani, embracing him tenderly. "Now I am sending my second self into the world. When you are tired and want rest, come back to me: old Wio-Wani will take you in."

Tiki-Pu was sobbing and the tears were running down his cheeks as he stepped out of Wio-Wani's wonderfully painted garden and stood once more upon earth. Turning, he saw the old man walking away along the path towards the little door under the palace-wall. At the door Wio-Wani turned and waved his hand for the last time. Tiki-Pu still stood watching him. Then the door opened and shut, and Wio-Wani was gone. Softly as a flower the picture seemed to have folded its leaves over him.

Tiki-Pu leaned a wet face against the picture and kissed the door in the palace-wall which Wio-Wani had painted so beautifully. "O Wio-Wani, dear master," he cried, "are you there?"

He waited, and called again, but no voice answered him.

Ali Baba and the Forty Thieves

———————————————*———————————————

Ali Baba was a poor woodcutter who lived in a small town in Persia very many years ago and who earned his living by selling his wood in the market-place.

One day as he was riding his mule through the forest on his way home, he saw an enormous cloud of dust which seemed to be moving towards him. As it got nearer it turned out to be a troop of horsemen, so Ali Baba got off his mule and climbed up into a tree to hide, fearing they might be robbers.

Robbers they were indeed, forty of them, and they rode past the tree where Ali was hiding, alighted from their horses outside a huge rock, and removed their saddle-bags, which seemed to be very heavy.

Then Ali Baba heard the man at the head of the troop (apparently the leader) call out in a loud voice the words, "Open Sesame," and to his great astonishment a huge door in the rock opened slowly and all forty robbers went inside carrying their loaded saddle-bags. Then the door slowly closed behind them. Ali was bursting with curiosity to see how long the robbers would remain in the cave. At last the door opened again, they all came out with empty saddle-bags, the leader said, "Shut Sesame" (at which the door closed), and they all mounted their horses, galloped off and were soon out of sight. Ali Baba came down from his hiding-place, walked up to the rock and called out, "Open Sesame," just as the robber chief had done. The door opened and in he went.

In front of him was a cavern, not dark as one might have expected but beautifully lit and filled to overflowing with all kinds of precious things—diamonds, rubies, jewels, bales of gorgeous silks, heavy, rich carpets and piles and piles of gold and silver coins.

Ali Baba was dazzled by the sight of all this wealth and concluded that it must be the result of years and years of theft and robbery by the forty men he had just seen and also perhaps by their fathers and grandfathers before them.

Ali Baba then loaded his own mule with as much riches as he possibly could and set off home, not forgetting to say, "Shut Sesame," before he left.

Ali Baba and the Forty Thieves

When he showed his wife all the gold, silver and jewels she was so overcome with delight and surprise that she wanted to tell all her neighbours about it. But Ali Baba said that nobody must be told. He decided to wait until nightfall and then dig a hole in his garden and bury all the precious things for the time being.

"But aren't you going to count it first?" asked his wife.

"There's far too much to count," replied Ali.

"Well let me at least borrow a measuring-jar so that we can measure it," insisted his wife. This was a most unusual idea, but Ali consented and so off she went to Ali's brother, Cassim, who was very rich and very mean and never did anything to help anyone, not even his poor brother.

Now Cassim happened to be out, but his wife, a very inquisitive creature, wondered what sort of grain it might be that her sister-in-law wanted to measure (not dreaming, of course, that it was money). So she placed a bit of sticky fat at the bottom of the measuring-jar so that some of the grain might cling to it without her sister-in-law noticing.

But when Ali's wife returned the jar, to Cassim's wife's great astonishment, it was not grain but a piece of gold that was sticking to the bit of fat.

"How very odd," she remarked. "Measuring gold, indeed! And he's supposed to be a poor woodcutter."

When the rich Cassim came back that night, his wife said to him:

"I have some news for you, husband. You have a very wealthy brother. So wealthy indeed that he needs a measuring-jar to measure his gold." The mean Cassim was smitten with envy and first thing next morning he burst into Ali's house shouting, "You pretend to be poor. Just explain this." And he held up the piece of gold stuck to the fat.

Ali, realizing that his wife had let out the secret, confessed everything and offered his brother part of the treasure.

"Oh no!" said Cassim, "you must tell me exactly where the

treasures are so that I can help myself when I choose. Otherwise I shall inform the authorities." So Ali Baba was forced to tell everything, even the magic words, "Open Sesame".

The very next day Cassim was off to the cavern with a dozen of his mules all laden with empty coffers and chests. Having arrived at the rock, he pronounced the words and the door opened. He went in and the door closed again. He filled as many bags of gold, silver and jewels as he could carry and laid them by the door and then called out, "Open . . ." but could not for the life of him think what the second word could be. Sesame, as you know, is the name of a grain and Cassim could think of every possible grain except the right one. He tried Open Barley, Open Wheat, Open Rye, and so on but, of course, nothing happened. The door remained stubbornly closed. His heart began to pound furiously, he got into a panic and forgot all about the enormous treasure he was going to take home.

At noon the robbers returned to the cavern and found Cassim's mules outside with all the chests and coffers on their backs. When the door opened at the leader's magic words Cassim rushed out and fell right into his arms. The robbers, in great fury, slew him without ceremony with their sabres and, as a lesson to any other would-be robber, they cut up his body into quarters and hung them outside the rock. It was indeed a most terrible spectacle.

Cassim's wife was very alarmed when her husband did not return that night. She ran to Ali Baba and begged him to go in search of him. So he set off with a couple of mules and when he got near the rock he was most alarmed to find drops of blood and almost collapsed when he saw the terrible remains of his mutilated brother. But, quickly recovering his composure, he loaded them on to the back of one of the mules and covered them over with wood and straw. The other mule he loaded with gold and also covered with straw. Then he rode back home.

Ali Baba and the Forty Thieves

He drove the mule laden with gold into his own yard and left his wife to unload it. The other one he led into the yard of his sister-in-law's house and knocked at her door. Luckily it was opened by Morgiana, Cassim's very intelligent slave. Ali Baba took her aside and whispered, "The cut-up remains of your master's body is in these two bundles on the mule. We must bury him as though he had died a natural death. I am trusting you to see that this is kept secret and to arrange for the burial." He then went indoors and consoled Cassim's distraught widow as best he could—no easy task, as you may well imagine.

Morgiana then went to a nearby apothecary's shop and asked for a drug to cure a most dangerous disease. "My master Cassim," she said, "is dangerously ill." She took the drug home but the next morning she was back once more at the apothecary's, begging him with tears in her eyes (and wailing in a loud voice so that everybody might hear) for some drastic drug for her dying master. That night, therefore, when crying and wailing were heard to come from Cassim's house, nobody was surprised at the news of his death.

The next day Morgiana went to a cobbler named Mustapha and said to him, "I will give you a piece of gold if you come with me, with your eyes blindfolded, to a certain place with your cobbler's needle and thread." Mustapha was suspicious at first, but when she offered him another piece of gold he went along with her to her late master's house. She did not uncover his eyes until they were in the room where the pieces of Cassim's body lay ready to be sewn together. "You must stitch the pieces to one another," she told him, "and then I will give you two more pieces of gold." Mustapha set to work (though with some reluctance and some distaste) and the task was soon done. Morgiana then blindfolded him and guided him home. The next day Cassim's funeral took place and everybody believed he had died of a sudden and rare disease. Thanks to the clever Morgiana, nobody remotely suspected what a horrible death he had really died. A few days later Ali Baba, with all his goods and family, moved into the widow's house.

Now when the forty thieves returned to their retreat you can imagine their surprise on finding Cassim's body removed and more treasures stolen.

"We must lose no time in finding out the man responsible for this," said their chief, "or we shall gradually lose all the wealth we and our grandfathers have accumulated over so many long years."

One robber immediately volunteered to go and spy out the town and find the man who was cheating them of their wealth.

"You are a brave man," said the captain, "but I must warn you that by our code of honour if you fail in your task you must pay with your life." The man readily agreed and the others applauded him for his courage. He disguised himself and set off to the town market. Purely by chance he happened to stop by Mustapha's cobbler's stall.

"You seem very old, my man," he said to him, "to have eyes keen enough to thread a needle."

"I am the best cobbler in this town," boasted Mustapha, "and only this very morning I stitched a dead body in a place that was not nearly as light as this market-square."

"Really?" said the robber in great astonishment. "I would very much like to see this place," and he offered him a piece of gold as an inducement.

"I am afraid I cannot lead you there, for I was blindfolded both to and from the house," replied Mustapha.

"Well, let me blindfold you," said the thief coaxingly, "and let us walk together a little way. Who knows, maybe you will manage to remember the way," and he pressed another gold piece into the cobbler's hand.

Having tied a handkerchief over Mustapha's eyes, the thief, partly guiding and partly being led, somehow contrived to get the cobbler to find Cassim's house (where, of course, Ali Baba now lived).

"Are you sure this is the right house?" asked the thief, having removed the handkerchief from Mustapha's eyes.

"I somehow feel this is as far as I came," was the reply, "but as I do not live in this part of the town I cannot say with certainty." However, the thief quickly made a mark with a piece of chalk on the door and returned to the forest to his chief.

Meanwhile Morgiana, returning from some errand, noticed

the chalk mark on the door. "How very odd," she remarked, "someone must be plotting some evil against my master," and the clever girl chalked the very same mark on three doors on either side of the house.

The robber had by now reported what he thought to be the success of his mission and the whole gang decided to enter the town that evening and make an end of their enemy. But imagine their utter dismay when, having arrived at Cassim's house, they found several doors identically marked. Their guide was dumbfounded and said he was prepared to die for having misled them.

No sooner was he slain than another chief volunteered and he too met Mustapha and was escorted to the same spot. He too marked the door, this time with red chalk at the bottom corner. But again the clever Morgiana noticed it and again chalk-marked several doors in the same spot with the same coloured chalk. And so the second guide had to pay with his life. The chief of the gang was by this time so furious that he decided to investigate the matter himself. He was led to the spot as before by Mustapha and he did *not* put a chalk mark on the door. He simply stared at it for a long time till he decided he could not possibly forget it. Then he summoned his thirty-seven thieves and ordered them to go to the village and buy nineteen mules with thirty-eight large leather jars—one full of oil and the others empty. The nineteen mules were then loaded with the thirty-seven robbers (in the jars!) and the jar of oil. The chief set out with them and drove them into the town just as dusk was falling. The chief rode up to Cassim's house and was just about to knock at the door when he caught sight of Ali Baba himself reclining outside after his supper. Addressing himself to Ali, the chief said: "I have come a long way to sell my oil in the market. Would you be so kind as to grant me hospitality for the night?" Ali welcomed him with his usual courtesy and warmth (not, of course, recognising him as the robber chief) and after they had eaten a plentiful meal they went to bed.

The chief, however, waited a few moments and then slipped back outside to where the mules were and as he passed from one to the other he raised the lid of the jars and whispered: "When I throw a few stones out of the window, come out quietly and I will join you." He then went back to the room which Ali had prepared for him.

Now it so happened that when Morgiana was preparing food for breakfast the lamp went out and it occurred to her that she might get some oil from one of the jars on the merchant's mules. Just as she was approaching the first jar she heard a voice saying, "Is it time yet?" "Aha," thought the clever slave girl, "more trouble! My master must be in grave danger." So with great presence of mind she whispered, "No, not yet awhile, but soon." And she said the same to all the jars—except, of course, the last one, for no voice came from that one, it being filled with oil. So she filled up her oil-pot, took it indoors, lit her lamp and went out again to the oil-jar with a kettle. This she filled with oil and set it to heat up on a large wood fire. As soon as it had boiled she poured some oil into every jar and thus destroyed the thirty-seven thieves one by one.

A second later she heard the sound of stones falling outside. This was the chief's signal that he was coming to join his gang. There was, of course, no reply—they were all dead. But when he came down and arrived at the last jar he guessed, from the oil that was missing, how they must have met their death. Furiously he rushed away, mounted his horse and escaped as fast as he could.

Next morning when Ali rose he was astonished to find the "merchant" gone but the mules with the oil-jars still there. He asked Morgiana whether she knew the reason for this. "Just follow me, my good master," she replied, "and you will see how

God has preserved you and your family." When Ali looked into the first jar and saw a man inside he shrank back in terror. "That man can do you no harm," said Morgiana. "He is dead and so are all his thirty-six comrades in the other jars." And she explained everything to Ali, showed him the nearly empty oil-jar and told him how important it was to keep the whole thing a secret from the neighbours.

"But what has happened to the merchant?" insisted Ali Baba. "That man is no more a merchant than I," replied the girl and she told the whole story from beginning to end, from the chalk-marking of the doors to the destruction of the robbers.

Ali Baba was overwhelmed with gratitude. "You have saved my life," he said, "and you have earned your freedom." Morgiana was overjoyed, but in her heart she felt her master still needed her.

Then, with the help of other servants, they dug a deep, long trench and buried the thieves. They carefully hid all the jars and weapons and, later, the mules were sold, one at a time so as not to arouse suspicion.

When the robber chief arrived back at the cavern he was at his wits' end. It was terrible to be there all alone without his thirty-nine followers. He made new plans for avenging himself upon Ali Baba and decided to open a shop near Cassim's, where he had heard that Ali's son now also had a shop. He conveyed rich carpets and silks and other precious goods there and set up business as a wealthy merchant. He became very friendly with Ali Baba's son, gave him many presents and invited him to dinner several times. Ali's son did not want to feel indebted to this rich and friendly man, so he asked his father whether he could invite him in return. Ali Baba replied, "By all means, my son. Bring him to my house tomorrow and a sumptuous repast will be prepared for him." The next evening Ali's son duly escorted the pretended merchant to his father's house but, strange to relate, as soon as they got to the door the merchant hesitated and was on the point of turning back. Just at that moment Ali Baba came forward, greeting him warmly and thanking him for the kindness he had shown to his son. "I am glad you are doing me the honour of dining with me," he said. "I would gladly," replied the pretended merchant, "but I have taken a vow not to eat salt and I therefore cannot sit at your table." (In eastern countries "to eat salt" at one's host's table is a sign of friendship.) "Pray do not concern yourself about that," said Ali Baba, "I shall ask the cook to put no salt in the food." Morgiana, in the kitchen, was much astonished to hear about this unusual request and very curious to see what manner of man it could be who would eat no salt. Under the pretence of helping to carry in the dishes she came up and saw the merchant and immediately identified him as the robber chief. As she passed close to him, her eagle eye perceived a small dagger concealed beneath his robe. The shrewd girl immediately thought of a plan to thwart the robber's evil designs on her master. She went down and disguised herself as a dancer and hung a small poniard to the delicate silver girdle round her waist. Then, accompanied by a slave musician playing the tabor, she danced her way into the dining-room. She danced with great beauty and grace, leaping and pirouetting unexpectedly, holding the poniard in her hand. At one moment she pointed it dangerously at her own breast but a second later she suddenly swerved over to where the merchant was seated and plunged it deep into his heart.

Ali Baba and his son were speechless with shock.

"Unhappy girl! What have you done! This will mean ruin for me and my family!" cried her master.

"Do not be angry, dear master," said Morgiana. "I have done this to save you." And pulling open the dead man's robe she revealed the dagger. "This is the chief of the forty thieves and also the false oil-merchant. Now you can understand why he would not eat salt at your table."

Once more Ali Baba was overcome with gratitude and joy. Morgiana had saved his life a second time.

"Not only will I give you your freedom," he said, "but I would also ask you to do us the honour of marrying my son." This was a very happy arrangement for all concerned and elaborate preparations were made for the wedding ceremony and marriage feast. At the wedding there was much banqueting, dancing and merrymaking and people talked about it for many years afterwards.

As for the "Open Sesame" cavern, Ali Baba taught his son the secret and it remained with the family for many generations, but they also used their great wealth to benefit others less fortunate than themselves.

The Bell of Atri

————————————————————*————————————————————

The city of Atri, tucked away in the Abruzzi mountains in Italy, was famous for two things—a bell and a horse.

When the bell was first hung up in the market-place in a lofty tower, the people were called together and the King made a speech in which he said:

"My friends, I have placed this bell right in the centre of the market-place of our city of Atri. It is within the reach of everyone, great or small, child, man or woman. But I must impress upon you that you may ring it only if you feel some wrong has been done to you. The rope is a very long one, so that even the very smallest child can pull it. I hope it will not have to be used very often."

The honest citizens of Atri listened respectfully and attentively. They were good folk and they knew that the need to use the bell would not arise very frequently.

Nevertheless, there it hung as a reminder to them all that they should be kind and just towards one another. In the first year it was rung only once, in the second year four times and during the next ten years only six times. This shows how well behaved the people of Atri were.

However, one day as the Mayor of the city was passing he noticed that the strands of the rope were fraying.

"My goodness," he told his secretary, "the rope is wearing

out. It must be due to the sun and the rain for, as you know, it has not been used very much. We shall have to get a new one."

"And how are we going to do that?" asked his secretary. "There is certainly no rope long enough in this town. The King had it specially woven in a village in Latium on the other side of the mountains. The only thing to do is to send over there for one to be made immediately."

"And what if somebody commits a wrong in the meantime?" asked the Mayor.

"Well now," replied his secretary. "I have a more than usually long grape-vine in my garden. We can fasten it to the bell. It should be sufficient for the time being, until the new rope is ready. And certainly quite tough enough, I'm positive."

The Mayor thought it was a good idea and so the bell was attached to the grape-vine.

Now a couple of miles outside Atri there lived a very rich old man. In his younger days he had been a soldier in many wars and had owned many horses. Gradually he had sold them all except one, which had been with him in many a fierce battle, and which he kept as a kind of souvenir of his adventurous youth. But a day came when the old man looked at his horse and said: "You are no good to me any more, old fellow. You're too old to work and I am not going to feed you any more. Out you go." So off limped the old horse and his cruel master bolted the gate behind him.

The poor old thing dragged his weary bones along for many hours, looking for bits of hay or patches of grass. He grew thinner and thinner and felt very, very miserable.

One day he hobbled into the town of Atri and came to the market-place, where his hungry eyes espied the grape-vine to which the great bell was tied.

He smacked his poor parched lips in eager anticipation of something good to eat at last. He trotted up and began to munch the green leaves. Then he tugged at it to get at the leaves growing higher up the vine.

"Ding-dong, ding-dong," pealed the great bell and people came hurrying out of their houses to see what was happening. You can imagine their amazement when they saw a poor old horse tugging at the grape-vine.

"I recognize that horse," said the Mayor's secretary (who seemed to know pretty well everything). "He belongs to that rich old soldier who lives outside the city."

"He must have got rid of the poor creature because it was too old to work," said the Mayor. "Summon him at once."

The old soldier was brought before the Mayor and, rather

shame-facedly, he admitted he had done his faithful horse a great wrong.

"Indeed you have," said the Mayor. "This good horse which served you so long and well in your adventurous youth you have now most ungratefully cast aside. This city orders you to take him back and give him a comfortable stall and to feed him properly for the rest of his days."

The crowd cheered to see justice done to man and beast alike and the old soldier, his head hanging down in shame, led his horse back home.

And that is why, as the poet Longfellow puts it:

> *. . . in every Christian clime*
> *The bell of Atri will be famous for all time.*

Jason and the Golden Fleece

————————————————————*————————————————————

In ancient Greece, many centuries ago, a certain King named
Aeson might have been seen wandering among the mountains with his young son, Jason. He had been driven from his
throne and kingdom of Iolcos by his cruel, tyrannical brother-
in-law, Pelias. After they had trudged many a long mile over
marshland and crag, up mountains and down steep valleys,
Aeson had to carry his son on his back and he was a very weary
man indeed when he at last arrived at a cave at the foot of a
mighty cliff where Chiron lived. Now Chiron was a Centaur and
like all the Centaurs he was a man down to the waist but below
he had the body of a noble horse. And Chiron was wiser and
kinder than anyone in the whole world. His white hair fell over
his broad shoulders and a long silvery beard half hid his massive
chest. Aeson left Jason with Chiron to be looked after and to be
brought up in the way a young prince should be brought up and
taught all the things a young prince should know. Many kings
before had sent their sons to Chiron, for there was nothing he
could not teach them. He was the finest player of the harp, he
was the deadliest archer, he sang the most haunting songs, he
could tell wondrous tales of olden times, and his skill with spear
and sword was unsurpassed.

The boy Jason was full of admiration and respect for this
amazing teacher and so here, with many other heroes and

princes, he grew up to be a strong, handsome young man well
versed in the arts of singing, dancing and playing the harp, and
skilled in hunting, riding and wrestling, and also in the art of
medicine and healing. He was later to become known as Jason
the Healer.

But now the time had come for Jason to leave the cave of
Chiron and to set out to punish the wicked Pelias for all the
wrong he had done to his father Aeson. So, bidding a sad farewell to his wise master, with a spear in each hand and a leopard's
skin flung over his shoulder, he set forth on his long travels. On
his feet were a pair of richly embroidered sandals, tied with
slender golden thongs, which had belonged to his father.

One day as he reached the foot of a lofty mountain he arrived
at a veritable raging torrent of a stream, swollen by heavy rains.
An old woman, with a peacock on her shoulder, stood on the
edge, not daring to cross. Jason, remembering Chiron's words

that the strong must help the weak, and although himself hesitant to step into those turbulent waters, offered to carry her across. The old woman was no light weight and Jason had to struggle furiously with the current dashing round his legs and thighs as he stumbled against trunks of trees uprooted by the mighty surge of the waters. His sandalled feet kept sticking to the muddy bed of the stream and just as he was about to reach the opposite bank one sandal left his foot, to be carried relentlessly away. Heaving a sigh of relief, he put the old woman carefully down, but imagine his astonishment when he saw that she had changed into the greatest of all goddesses, Hera, the wife of Zeus. With a promise to help him wherever he went she vanished into thin air, leaving Jason standing there, drenched to the skin, with only one sandal, and breathless with wonder.

Limping wearily on he came at long last to the city of Iolcos. People stopped in the streets to stare at this strange handsome youth with his leopard skin. But when they looked at his feet they began to whisper, "Look, he wears only one sandal." The whispers grew to a murmur and very soon you could hear one single cry from all sides, "The man with one sandal has come. The man with one sandal has come." When the King heard of his arrival he trembled with fear, for it had been foretold that one day a man wearing only one sandal would come and take away his kingdom. However, he made a great pretence of being pleased to see the stranger and told him he was the very man he had been waiting for. He needed a strong, brave man, daring enough to go to Colchis to bring back the Golden Fleece.

Now Jason knew all about the Golden Fleece. It had come from the back of a wonderful gold-fleeced ram which had saved two children, Phryxus and Helle, from the clutches of their stepmother, who wanted to kill them. The ram had flown away with the two, carrying them on its back. The girl, Helle, had fallen into the sea (which later became known as the Hellespont) but Phryxus had reached Colchis and hung the fleece on the branch of an oak tree, where it lit up the dark woods and shone with a golden light for many miles around. It was now guarded by a terrible sleepless dragon in the royal grove at Colchis. Many heroes had tried in vain to capture the Golden Fleece. To go in quest of it was like marching to certain death. Jason knew all this full well and he knew that the cunning King Pelias hoped to get rid of him by suggesting that he should go and capture it. At that very instant he could hear the voice of the great goddess Hera (that same goddess, who, disguised as an old woman, had tested his courage and kindness by asking him to carry her across the turbulent stream) whisper to him, "Be not afraid, Jason, I shall help you." So he looked King Pelias straight in the eye and said calmly, "I will go and capture the Golden Fleece and will bring it back here to this palace—or perish in the attempt—but on one condition."

"And what is that condition, Jason?" asked the King.

"That you return to my father his rightful kingdom," was Jason's reply.

"I will. I swear most solemnly that I will," said the King loudly, but inwardly he thought, "Well, that is the end of him," and he smiled to himself at the clever way he thought he had trapped the brave youth into undertaking this dread mission.

The first thing Jason did when he rose next morning at the break of dawn was to ask the advice of the enchanted tree known as the Talking Oak which stood towering, over a hundred feet high, in the centre of an ancient wood in Dodona.

"What must I do," he asked, "to gain the Golden Fleece?" Through the myriads of rustling leaves Jason heard the clear reply:

"Go to Argus the Shipbuilder and ask him to build you a galley with fifty oars." In the city of Iolchos Jason did indeed find this famed shipwright, who immediately set to work, helped

Jason and the Golden Fleece

by innumerable apprentices. When the ship, the *Argo*, was completed, people came from far and wide to admire it, for no ship so large and heavy had ever been built before. Then Jason went once more to ask the advice of the Talking Oak. This time it told him to hack off one of its boughs and to have it carved into a figurehead for the *Argo*. When it was finished Jason was surprised to hear a voice coming from the mouth of the figurehead.

"Send out heralds," said the voice, "to all the heroes and princes who were your schoolmates and playfellows in Chiron's cave and get forty-nine of them to accompany you in your quest for the Golden Fleece."

So messengers were dispatched throughout all the cities and towns of Greece.

"Who will dare", cried the messengers, "who will dare help Jason row his vessel and be bold enough to face dangers too terrible to describe and bring back the Golden Fleece to Iolchos?"

Every youth with spirit was eager to take on this impossible quest, but Jason could select only forty-nine who had already proved themselves in dangerous combat. Among them were the mighty Hercules, Theseus, and the twins Castor and Pollux, and Orpheus, who played on his lyre and sang with such haunting charm that the wildest of beasts would sit down tamely before him and stare dreamily into the distance. And there were times when he played more stirring tunes and then whole forests of trees would uproot themselves and great rocks and boulders would come careering madly down the hills.

Now they were ready to launch the *Argo* down the beach, but she proved too heavy for even them to move and her keel sank into the sand. So once more Jason had to ask the advice of the magic figurehead—the bough of the Talking Oak.

"Let Orpheus play gently upon the lyre," said the figurehead. So the heroes waited and held the pine-trunk rollers firmly while

Jason and the Golden Fleece

Orpheus played and sang. And lo! gradually there was a stirring in all the ship's timbers, and then a mighty heaving from stem to stern and finally the *Argo* sprang on to the rollers and leapt forward into the surging sea. And so the good ship *Argo* was launched.

Then, having provided her well with food and water, they all took their places at the oars and rowed away to the shouting and cheering of the people watching from the cliff tops.

The first stop on their voyage was at the cave of Chiron, their old master, who gave them his blessing and good advice. Soon they were to meet their first peril, the dreaded rocks of the Black Sea, which actually moved and crashed into one another, ready to crush all comers. They waited in vain for an opening in the rocks and it seemed that they would never get through. Then suddenly a heron came flying mast-high towards the rocks and hovered and soared around for a while as though waiting for a passage through. Jason realized that the bird had been sent to them by Hera to act as a pilot. They saw the heron fly swiftly through in safety just as the mighty rocks came crashing together and caught a feather from its tail. Then the rocks parted as if riven asunder by the shock of the collision and now our heroes bent over their oars with all their might and rowed safely through before the rocks could come together again.

And now they rowed further and further eastward along the southern shores of the Euxine Sea and after many more breath-taking perils and adventures and many a narrow escape from death, the Argonauts espied in the distance the gleaming gold of the palace of King Aietes in the city of Colchis where, hidden among the woods, was the Golden Fleece.

The King was told of their approach and he came down to the riverside in his golden chariot, followed by a train of servants and fierce-looking soldiers. He was a splendid sight, this Child of the Sun, in robes of heavy gold tissue and with the jewels of his crown flashing fire. He did indeed look like his father, the sun himself.

But Jason and his heroes were not afraid.

"We have not come to plunder your land," Jason said calmly to the King, "but to take back the Golden Fleece to Iolchos. If you wish to fight us, then fight we must, but I must warn you that my comrades are heroes of great renown and that some are sons of the Immortals."

Much to Jason's surprise, Aietes's reply was mild. "Why should we fight?" he asked. "Far better to choose one of your best men and let him carry out the duties I will require of him. If he is successful, I shall give him the opportunity to win the Golden Fleece."

Jason, as leader of the Argonauts, accepted the challenge for himself, but little did he imagine what he would have to achieve to gain his objective.

First, he must tame two fire-eating bulls and plough a four-acre field with them.

Second, he must sow that field with a dragon's teeth, which would immediately spring up into fully-armed men.

Third, he must fight and conquer these armed warriors.

Now, Aietes's beautiful daughter, Medea, who was also an enchantress, had fallen in love with Jason as soon as she had set eyes on him. She did not want him to die. So that evening she sent a messenger-boy to the shore where Jason, with his men, was keeping watch over their good ship the *Argo*.

"Go quickly to the Palace," whispered the lad to Jason, "where the Princess Medea wishes to speak with you urgently."

When Jason saw the Princess he felt he was in the presence of someone who was both very beautiful and very terrible.

"Jason," she said, "if you trust me and if you are indeed fearless, I can tell you how to tame the fiery bulls, sow the dragon's teeth and win the Golden Fleece. For I am an enchantress and

Jason and the Golden Fleece

I know all about the old woman you carried across the stream, the Talking Oak and the adventures you have had in coming to Colchis." Jason listened eagerly, quite overwhelmed by the Princess's beauty.

"Here is a charmed ointment," continued Medea, handing him a golden box. "If you smear this over your body the bulls' fiery breath cannot harm you." She then handed him a basket containing the dragon's teeth and led him to the field where the bulls were quietly grazing. As Medea left him, Jason tiptoed nearer and nearer to the bulls, and he could clearly see four streams of fiery vapour oozing out from their nostrils. He halted and smeared his body with the enchanted ointment and went boldly on. Hearing his footsteps the bulls sprang up with a fierce roar and came charging towards him, their breath scorching the pasture before them. But the heat did not touch Jason and his heart was brave. Just as they were about to toss him high up into the air, he grabbed one of them by the horn and the other by the tail and held them in a grip of iron. And suddenly they were just ordinary bulls, breathing in the ordinary way. Jason's courage and Medea's ointment had broken the spell. Jason then yoked the bulls, harnessed them to the plough lying in a corner of the field and ploughed the whole field in the expert way that his master Chiron had taught him. He then scattered the dragon's teeth far and wide over the ploughed black earth and immediately there began to sprout up, helmets first, dark, fierce-looking warriors, one for each tooth. They formed ranks and charged as one man towards Jason, brandishing their flaming swords.

"Pick up a stone and throw it among them," called Medea's voice from the distance. This Jason did and the stone bounded off the helmet of one warrior and crashed into another's. Then there was complete confusion among them and instead of attacking Jason they all began fighting one another. And that was how Jason left them.

Jason and the Golden Fleece

Early next morning he went to the Palace of Aietes and told the King that he had tamed the fiery bulls, ploughed the field, sown the dragon's teeth and left the armed warriors killing one another. This put the King in a state of extreme terror, for he realized at once that his beautiful enchantress daughter had helped Jason to achieve all this and that now Jason would be perfectly capable of slaying the Dragon which guarded the Golden Fleece.

"You have not acted fairly," he said sternly to Jason. "And so I cannot allow you to try to win the Fleece."

As Jason was leaving the Palace, wondering what to do next, he was stopped by Medea. "Jason," she said, "my father has decreed that I must die. He also plans to burn your fine galley and to slay all your comrades. But if you trust me I shall help you. Wait for me here at midnight."

Jason replied: "You shall not die. We shall win the Golden Fleece and you will return with me to be my Queen in Iolcos by the sea."

At the appointed hour the pair made their way stealthily towards the Sacred Grove. Suddenly Jason stopped with a gasp of amazement. He had caught his first glimpse of the dazzling radiance of the Golden Fleece. So eager was he to see its full splendour that he would have rushed forward had not Medea held his arm. "Beware!" she warned, "have you forgotten the dragon?" It was at that moment that the scaly black head of the dreaded monster came into view, its forked tongue darting and hissing as it heard their footsteps. Medea drew out a gold box from the folds of her dress and flung its contents straight into the dragon's steaming jaws. With a furious flick of its enormous tail the beast surged forward and—fell motionless. Jason leapt lightly forward over the dragon's body and pulled the Golden Fleece from the tree. Then he and Medea rushed back to the shore where the *Argo* was beached, and they all made merry with

food and wine to celebrate their great capture. But their rejoic-
ings were soon cut short by the voice of the figurehead on the
Argo.

"Make haste, Jason," it said, "make haste, flee for your lives."
Jason looked up and saw the glittering chariot of Aietes, followed by innumerable warriors, speeding down towards the
shore. As one man all fifty heroes leapt to their oars as Jason
held aloft the wondrous Golden Fleece. Aietes and his men
hurled poisoned arrows in impotent rage at the scudding gal-
leon. But the Argonauts warded them off with their shields and
Orpheus took up his lyre and sang a song of praise to the heroes.
And to this sweet music the good ship *Argo* sped westwards
towards Iolcos to claim the kingdom for Jason and his queen.

Master of All Masters

———————————— * ————————————

A girl once went to the fair to hire herself for servant. At last a funny-looking old gentleman engaged her, and took her home to his house. When she got there, he told her that he had something to teach her, for that in his house he had his own names for things.

He said to her: "What will you call me?"

"Master or mister, or whatever you please, sir," says she.

He said: "You must call me 'master of all masters'. And what would you call this?" pointing to his bed.

"Bed or couch, or whatever you please, sir."

"No, that's my 'barnacle'. And what do you call these?" said he, pointing to his pantaloons.

"Breeches or trousers, or whatever you please, sir."

"You must call them 'squibs and crackers'. And what would you call her?" pointing to the cat.

"Cat or kit, or whatever you please, sir."

"You must call her 'white-faced simminy'. And this now," showing the fire, "what would you call this?"

"Fire or flame, or whatever you please, sir."

"You must call it 'hot cockalorum', and what this?" he went on, pointing to the water.

"Water or wet, or whatever you please, sir."

"No, 'pondalorum' is its name. And what do you call all this?" asked he, as he pointed to the house.

"House or cottage, or whatever you please, sir."

"You must call it 'high topper mountain'."

That very night the servant woke her master up in a fright and said: "Master of all masters, get out of your barnacle and put on

your squibs and crackers. For white-faced simminy has got a spark of hot cockalorum on its tail, and unless you get some pondalorum high topper mountain will be all on hot cockalorum."

　　　　　　　　　　　. . . That's all.

Many Moons

--------------------------------*--------------------------------

Once upon a time, in a kingdom by the sea, there lived a little Princess named Lenore. She was ten years old, going on eleven. One day Lenore fell ill of a surfeit of raspberry tarts and took to her bed.

The Royal Physician came to see her and took her temperature and felt her pulse and made her stick out her tongue. The Royal Physician was worried. He sent for the King, Lenore's father, and the King came to see her.

"I will get you anything your heart desires," the King said. "Is there anything your heart desires?"

"Yes," said the Princess. "I want the moon. If I can have the moon, I will be well again."

Now, the King had a great many wise men who always got for him anything he wanted, so he told his daughter that she could have the moon. Then he went to the throne room and pulled a bell cord, three long pulls and a short pull, and presently the Lord High Chamberlain came into the room.

The Lord High Chamberlain was a large, fat man who wore thick glasses which made his eyes seem twice as big as they really were. This made the Lord High Chamberlain seem twice as wise as he really was.

"I want to get the moon," said the King. "The Princess Lenore wants the moon. If she can have the moon, she will get well again."

"The moon?" exclaimed the Lord High Chamberlain, his eyes widening. This made him look four times as wise as he really was.

"Yes, the moon," said the King. "M-o-o-n, moon. Get it tonight, tomorrow at the latest."

The Lord High Chamberlain wiped his forehead with a handkerchief and then blew his nose loudly. "I have got a great many things for you in my time, Your Majesty," he said. "It just happens that I have with me a list of the things I have got for you in my time." He pulled a long scroll of parchment out of his pocket, "Let me see, now." He glanced at the list, frowning. "I have got ivory, apes, and peacocks, rubies, opals, and emeralds, black orchids, pink elephants, and blue poodles, gold bugs, scarabs, and flies in amber, humming-birds' tongues, angels' feathers, and unicorns' horns, giants, midgets, and mermaids, frankincense, ambergris, and myrrh, troubadours, minstrels, and dancing women, a pound of butter, two dozen eggs, and a sack of sugar—sorry, my wife wrote that in there."

"I don't remember any blue poodles," said the King.

"It says blue poodles right here on the list, and they are checked off with a little check mark," said the Lord High Chamberlain. "So that must have been blue poodles. You just forget."

"Never mind the blue poodles," said the King. "What I want now is the moon."

"I have sent as far as Samarkand and Araby and Zanzibar to

get things for you, Your Majesty," said the Lord High Chamberlain. "But the moon is out of the question. It is thirty-five thousand miles away and it is bigger than the room the Princess lies in. Furthermore, it is made of molten copper. I cannot get the moon for you. Blue poodles, yes; the moon, no."

The King flew into a rage and told the Lord High Chamberlain to leave the room and to send the Royal Wizard to the throne room.

The Royal Wizard was a little, thin man with a long face. He wore a high red peaked hat covered with silver stars, and a long blue robe covered with golden owls. His face grew very pale when the King told him that he wanted the moon for his little daughter, and that he expected the Royal Wizard to get it.

"I have worked a great deal of magic for you in my time, Your Majesty," said the Royal Wizard. "As a matter of fact, I just happen to have in my pocket a list of the wizardries I have performed for you." He drew a paper from a deep pocket of his robe. "It begins: Dear Royal Wizard: I am returning herewith the so-called philosopher's stone which you claimed—no, that isn't it." The Royal Wizard brought a long scroll of parchment from another pocket of his robe. "Here it is," he said. "Now, let's see. I have squeezed blood out of turnips for you, and turnips out of blood. I have produced rabbits out of silk hats, and silk hats out of rabbits. I have conjured up flowers, tambourines, and doves out of nowhere, and nowhere out of flowers, tambourines, and doves. I have brought you divining rods, magic wands, and crystal spheres in which to behold the future. I have compounded philtres, unguents, and potions, to cure heartbreak, surfeit, and ringing in the ears. I have made you my own special mixture of wolfbane, nightshade, and eagles' tears, to ward off witches, demons, and things that go bump in the night. I have given you seven-league boots, the golden touch, and a cloak of invisibility——"

93

"It didn't work," said the King. "The cloak of invisibility didn't work."

"Yes, it did," said the Royal Wizard.

"No, it didn't," said the King. "I kept bumping into things, the same as ever."

"The cloak is supposed to make you invisible," said the Royal Wizard. "It is not supposed to keep you from bumping into things."

"All I know is, I kept bumping into things," said the King.

The Royal Wizard looked at his list again. "I got you," he said, "horns from Elfland, sand from the Sandman, and gold from the rainbow. Also a spool of thread, a paper of needles, and a lump of beeswax—sorry, those are things my wife wrote down for me to get her."

"What I want you to do now," said the King, "is to get me the moon. The Princess Lenore wants the moon, and when she gets it she will be well again."

"Nobody can get the moon," said the Royal Wizard. "It is a hundred and fifty thousand miles away, and it is made of green cheese, and it is twice as big as this palace."

The King flew into another rage and sent the Royal Wizard back to his cave. Then he rang a gong and summoned the Royal Mathematician.

The Royal Mathematician was a bald-headed, near-sighted man, with a skull-cap on his head and a pencil behind each ear. He wore a black suit with white numbers on it.

"I don't want to hear a long list of all the things you have figured out for me since 1907," the King said to him. "I want you to figure out right now how to get the moon for the Princess Lenore. When she gets the moon, she will be well again."

"I am glad you mentioned all the things I have figured out for you since 1907," said the Royal Mathematician. "It so happens that I have a list of them with me."

Many Moons

He pulled a long scroll of parchment out of a pocket and looked at it. "Now, let me see. I have figured out for you the distance between the horns of a dilemma, night and day, and A and Z. I have computed how far is Up, how long it takes to get to Away, and what becomes of Gone. I have discovered the length of the sea serpent, the price of the priceless and the square of the hippopotamus. I know where you are when you are at Sixes and Sevens, how much Is you have to have to make an Are, and how many birds you can catch with the salt in the ocean— 187,796,132, if it would interest you to know."

"There aren't many birds," said the King.

"I didn't say there were," said the Royal Mathematician. "I said if there were."

"I don't want to hear about seven hundred million imaginary birds," said the King. "I want you to get the moon for the Princess Lenore."

"The moon is three hundred thousand miles away," said the Royal Mathematician. "It is round and flat like a coin, only it is made of asbestos, and it is half the size of this kingdom. Furthermore, it is pasted on the sky. Nobody can get the moon."

The King flew into still another rage and sent the Royal Mathematician away. Then he rang for the Court Jester. The jester came bounding into the throne room in his motley and his cap and bells, and sat at the foot of the throne.

"What can I do for you, Your Majesty?" asked the Court Jester.

"Nobody can do anything for me," said the King mournfully. "The Princess wants the moon, and she cannot be well till she gets it, but nobody can get it for her. Every time I ask anybody for the moon, it gets larger and farther away. There is nothing you can do for me except play on your lute. Something sad."

"How big do they say the moon is," asked the Court Jester, "and how far away?"

"The Lord High Chamberlain says it is thirty-five thousand miles away, and bigger than the Princess Lenore's room," said the King. "The Royal Wizard says it is a hundred and fifty thousand miles away, and twice as big as this palace. The Royal Mathematician says it is three thousand miles away, and half the size of this kingdom."

The Court Jester strummed on his lute for a little while. "They are all wise men," he said, "and so they must all be right. If they are all right, then the moon must be just as large and as far away as each person thinks it is. The thing to do is find out how big the Princess Lenore thinks it is, and how far away."

"I never thought of that," said the King.

"I will go and ask her, Your Majesty," said the Court Jester. And he crept very softly into the little girl's room.

The Princess Lenore was awake, and she was glad to see the Court Jester, but her face was very pale and her voice very weak.

"Have you brought the moon to me?" she asked.

"Not yet," said the Court Jester, "but I will get it for you right away. How big do you think it is?"

"It is just a little smaller than my thumb-nail," she said, "for when I hold my thumb-nail up at the moon, it just covers it."

"And how far away is it?" asked the Court Jester.

"It is not as high as the big tree outside my window," said the Princess, "for sometimes it gets caught in the top branches."

"It will be very easy to get the moon for you," said the Court Jester. "I will climb the tree tonight when it gets caught at the top branches and bring it to you."

Then he thought of something else. "What is the moon made of, Princess?" he asked.

"Oh," she said, "it's made of gold, of course, silly."

The Court Jester left the Princess Lenore's room and went to see the Royal Goldsmith. He had the Royal Goldsmith make a tiny round golden moon just a little smaller than the thumb-nail of the Princess Lenore. Then he had him string it on a golden chain so the Princess could wear it around her neck.

"What is this thing I have made?" asked the Royal Goldsmith when he had finished it.

"You have made the moon," said the Court Jester. "That is the moon."

"But the moon," said the Royal Goldsmith, "is five hundred thousand miles away and is made of bronze and is round like a marble."

"That's what you think," said the Court Jester as he went away with the moon.

The Court Jester took the moon to the Princess Lenore, and

97

she was overjoyed. The next day she was well again and could get up and go out in the garden to play.

But the King's worries were not yet over. He knew that the moon would shine in the sky again that night, and he did not want the Princess to see it. If she did, she would know that the moon she wore on a chain around her neck was not the real moon.

So the King sent for the Lord High Chamberlain and said, "We must keep the Princess Lenore from seeing the moon when it shines in the sky tonight. Think of something."

The Lord High Chamberlain tapped his forehead with his fingers thoughtfully and said, "I know just the thing. We can make some dark glasses for the Princess Lenore. We can make them so dark that she will not be able to see anything at all through them. Then she will not be able to see the moon when it shines in the sky."

This made the King very angry, and he shook his head from side to side. "If she wore dark glasses she would bump into things," he said, "and then she would be ill again." So he sent the Lord High Chamberlain away and called the Royal Wizard.

"We must hide the moon," said the King, "so that the Princess Lenore will not see it when it shines in the sky tonight. How are we going to do that?"

The Royal Wizard stood on his hands and then he stood on his head and then he stood on his feet again. "I know what we can do," he said. "We can stretch some black velvet curtains on poles. The curtains will cover all the palace gardens like a circus tent, and the Princess Lenore will not be able to see through them, so she will not see the moon in the sky."

The King was so angry at this that he waved his arms around. "Black velvet curtains would keep out the air," he said. "The Princess Lenore would not be able to breathe, and she would be ill again." So he sent the Royal Wizard away and summoned the Royal Mathematician.

Many Moons

"We must do something," said the King, "so that the Princess Lenore will not see the moon when it shines in the sky tonight. If you know so much, figure out a way to do that."

The Royal Mathematician walked around in a circle, and then he walked around in a square, and then he stood still. "I have it!" he said. "We can set off fireworks in the gardens every night. We will make a lot of silver fountains and golden cascades, and when they go off, they will fill the sky with so many sparks that it will be as light as day and the Princess Lenore will not be able to see the moon."

The King flew into such a rage that he began jumping up and down. "Fireworks would keep the Princess Lenore awake," he said. "She would not get any sleep at all and she would be ill again." So the King sent the Royal Mathematician away.

When he looked up again, it was dark outside and he saw the bright rim of the moon just peeping over the horizon. He jumped up in a great fright and rang for the Court Jester. The Court Jester came bounding into the room and sat down at the foot of the throne.

"What can I do for you, Your Majesty?" he asked.

"Nobody can do anything for me," said the King, mournfully. "The moon is coming up again. It will shine into the Princess Lenore's bedroom, and she will know it is still in the sky and that she does not wear it on a golden chain around her neck. Play me something on your lute, something very sad, for when the Princess sees the moon, she will be ill again."

The Court Jester strummed on his lute. "What do your wise men say?" he asked.

"They can think of no way to hide the moon that will not make the Princess Lenore ill," said the King.

The Court Jester played another song, very softly. "Your wise men know everything," he said, "and if they cannot hide the moon, then it cannot be hidden."

The King put his head in his hands again and sighed. Suddenly he jumped up from his throne and pointed to the windows. "Look!" he cried. "The moon is already shining into the Princess Lenore's bedroom. Who can explain how the moon can be shining in the sky when it is hanging on a golden chain around her neck?"

The Court Jester stopped playing on his lute. "Who could explain how to get the moon when your wise men said it was too large and too far away? It was the Princess Lenore. Therefore the Princess Lenore is wiser than your wise men and knows more about the moon than they do. So I will ask her." And before the King could stop him, the Court Jester slipped quietly out of the throne room and up the wide marble staircase to the Princess Lenore's bedroom.

The Princess was lying in bed, but she was wide awake and she was looking out of the window at the moon shining in the sky. Shining in her hand was the moon the Court Jester had got for her. He looked very sad, and there seemed to be tears in his eyes.

"Tell me, Princess Lenore," he said mournfully, "how can the moon be shining in the sky when it is hanging on a golden chain around your neck?"

The Princess looked at him and laughed. "That is easy, silly," she said. "When I lose a tooth, a new one grows in its place, doesn't it?"

"Of course," said the Court Jester. "And when the unicorn loses his horn in the forest, a new one grows in the middle of his forehead."

"That is right," said the Princess, "and when the Royal Gardener cuts the flowers in the garden, other flowers come to take their place."

"I should have thought of that," said the Court Jester, "for it is the same way with the daylight."

"And it is the same way with the moon," said the Princess Lenore. "I guess it is the same way with everything." Her voice became very low and faded away, and the Court Jester saw that she was asleep. Gently he tucked the covers in around the sleeping Princess.

But before he left the room, he went over to the window and winked at the moon, for it seemed to the Court Jester that the moon had winked back at him.

The Crocodile and the Monkey

————————————*————————————

There was once a crocodile who lived on a sandbank in a river. He was quite a nice fellow, sociable and affectionate, though not very clever. His wife, on the other hand, was not at all a nice person. She was, I am sorry to tell you, cruel, selfish, and vain, and of a very jealous disposition. In spite of this, her husband adored her. He even made poems to her.

They weren't particularly good poems; but it isn't very easy to make good poems, as everyone knows who has tried. But they weren't bad, for a crocodile. And I told you he wasn't very brainy. Here is one of the poems he made:

> *My beauteous one, my beauteous one,*
> *My croco—croco dear,*
> *By land or sea, where e'er it be*
> *You have no single peer.*
>
> *Your graceful form, your melting eyes,*
> *My loving heart beguile,*
> *I've searched around, no charm I've found*
> *To match your darling smile.*

When he told this to his wife she didn't look as pleased as you might have expected.

The Crocodile and the Monkey

"I don't like that last bit," she said; "the bit about searching around."

"No, I don't think that is a very good bit," said her husband. "I had a lot of difficulty over the last line but one. It sounds a little awkward, doesn't it? It wouldn't flow."

"I don't mind about the flow," said his wife. "It's the searching around I don't like, I tell you. You've no business to be searching around for a better smile than mine."

It was no use her husband trying to explain that he put that in to make a rhyme. Mrs. Crocodile wouldn't look at it that way, and though he changed the lines to:

> But oh, how fair, how sweet and rare
> Your darling, darling smile.

that made no difference. She kept on brooding over it and turning it over in her mind long after he had forgotten all about it.

The crocodile's wife was a lazy creature; she never moved about much, but spent most of her time idly basking in the sun and admiring her own reflection in the water. The crocodile, though, was rather energetic, and would go quite a long way in search of adventure. She always made him tell her exactly where he had been—he had to give an account of every single minute. This he always did most faithfully and truly, for he really had a very sincere nature.

One day, on one of his expeditions, he came to a place in the river where a fine banyan tree stood on the bank. He was hot and tired, and he lay down in the shallow water near the bank and rested. The banyan tree cast a pleasant shade, which he found very agreeable. Presently he noticed a monkey in the branches of the tree busy picking and eating the ripe fruit.

"Good morning," said the crocodile, when the monkey came down to a lower branch within speaking distance; "you seem to be enjoying yourself."

The Crocodile and the Monkey

"Good morning to you, sir," replied the monkey. "I'm enjoying myself very much indeed. Would you like some fruit? There's plenty here for both of us."

The crocodile thanked him politely, and the monkey threw down some of the ripe fruit for him to eat. They had a little more amiable conversation, and then the crocodile bade the monkey farewell and went off home to his wife, to whom, as usual, he told the story of his morning's adventure.

Before many days had gone by he went again to the same spot and again saw the monkey in the banyan tree. This he felt to be very fortunate, as he had so much enjoyed meeting him before. They had another pleasant talk, and again the crocodile very much appreciated the fruit which the monkey threw down to him. It was indeed a very great treat, for crocodiles, being unable to climb trees, are not able to get fruit for themselves.

When the time came for the crocodile to depart, the monkey said he hoped they would meet again.

"I am generally here in the mornings," he said, "and shall always be delighted to see you."

The crocodile promised to come again soon, which he did, and so, in a short time quite a warm friendship sprang up between the two.

The crocodile told his new friend all about his lovely wife, and the monkey on several occasions sent her a present of banyan fruit. The monkey told the crocodile all about his own affairs and his many adventures among the forest trees, which could be seen not very far away, and what with one thing and another they spent many happy hours together.

But as time went on the crocodile's wife became suspicious of this new friendship.

"I've searched around"—she kept repeating over and over again to herself. "That's what he's been doing—searching around. I don't believe a word of what he says. Probably that monkey doesn't even exist. He's spending his time with someone else!"

She gradually worked herself up into a great state over this, but, being a cunning as well as a jealous creature, she decided not to tell her husband her thoughts until she had contrived some means of putting an end to this friendship of which she was so suspicious. Finally she decided on a plan, and as a first step she pretended to be very ill; so one day, when her husband came home, he found her lying on the sandbank groaning and lamenting.

He was, of course, very much upset by this. He was afraid his beautiful and adored wife was going to die. She was, by the way, a very good actress and certainly had every appearance of being very ill indeed. He suggested all sorts of remedies, but she would have none of them.

At last, when he was in utter despair, she said, interrupting her remarks with many groans, that she had once heard a very learned person say that the heart of a monkey was a certain cure for that very malady from which she was suffering.

"But how am I to procure such a thing?" asked the anxious husband.

"That is easy enough," said his groaning wife. "What about your friend in the banyan tree? You could easily persuade him to give you his heart if you put your mind to it."

Her husband was horrified at the suggestion, as well he might be. Moreover, he was quite sure that the monkey would never consent to give him his heart, and said so. But his artful wife had a plan all ready in her head.

"There is no need at all for you to let him know that you want his heart," she said, "since you love me so little that you do not care to ask him for it. If you do as I tell you we can get him to come here without any difficulty, and once he is here and in our power we can do with him what we will."

The Crocodile and the Monkey

The crocodile was more upset than ever when he heard his wife's cunning suggestion as to how the monkey was to be tricked into coming. He spoke of the kind way in which the monkey had always behaved and pointed out with great earnestness that nothing in the whole world was so hateful as the betrayal of a friend. But his wife would not listen to him. She was determined to put an end to this business and to destroy this rival, whoever it might be.

She groaned and moaned and rolled about and wept bitterly, declaring that he loved his friend better than his wife, and that he would be glad if she died so that he could be more free to spend his time with the monkey.

"You have been searching around," she said. "I guessed it some time ago and now I know it for certain. It is that which has made me fall a victim to this terrible illness. But you do not care. You no longer love me, that is the truth of the matter. Oh . . . oh. . . . You will not have much longer to wait. Oh—oh—oh. . . ." And she writhed about in apparent agony.

The poor crocodile was at his wits' end. What could he do? He still adored his horrid wife, strange though it seems, and he really believed she was terribly ill.

So at last, very reluctantly, and with many misgivings, he promised to do what she wished. She thereupon gave him careful instructions as to how he must act in order to get the monkey to visit them, and he set off with a heavy heart.

The monkey was in the banyan tree as usual, happily jumping from branch to branch in the hot sunshine. When they had exchanged greetings and had had a little more pleasant talk, the crocodile felt that he could put off the evil moment no longer.

"I have a message for you from my wife," he said at last. "I have told her so much about you that she is dying to meet you. Moreover, she says I have been sadly wanting in hospitality

never to have asked you to come and see us after your great
kindness in the matter of the fruit. Will you not come back with
me today and pay us a visit?"

"That is very kind of you," said the monkey, "and I should
very much like to meet your wife, who, if she is as lovely as your
description of her, must indeed be beautiful. But how am I to
accompany you? I cannot swim; also I believe your home is in
the water and I cannot breathe under water."

"That is quite easy," said the crocodile, "we live on a sandbank, where you will be quite comfortable. As for getting there,
you have only to get on my back and I will convey you."

So the monkey accepted.

The crocodile's heart grew heavier and heavier. He was
touched at the monkey's trust in him, which he was about to
requite so hatefully. At the same time he kept thinking of his
sick wife and how she would certainly die if he returned without
the monkey.

The worst thing of all, it seemed to him, was the fact that the
monkey would have to die without preparing as he should to
meet his Maker.

He swam silently down the river, and the monkey, noticing
this, asked him what he was thinking about. So then, feeling that
the monkey could not possibly escape, for the river was wide and
he kept well to the middle of it, he told him of the fate in store
for him.

The monkey listened quietly until the crocodile had finished
and then replied: "My dear friend, I have heard your tale with
great sympathy and am very much touched by your unhappy
situation. Willingly will I give you my heart in order to save the
life of so beautiful a creature as your wife. But it is a pity you did
not tell me before we started on this journey. I have a habit of
hanging my heart every morning early on a branch of the banyan
tree so that it should not get damaged while I am jumping

about. However, the matter can easily be put right. If you will turn round and take me back I will get my heart for you."

So the crocodile, after earnestly thanking the monkey, swam back again to the place whence they had started. And as soon as they drew in to the bank the monkey leaped off the crocodile's back and up into the tree, and looked down at the crocodile, who was expectantly waiting close to the bank.

"Go back to your horrid wife, you silly old crocodile," said the monkey, "and tell her that monkeys may keep their hearts hanging on branches, but they keep their wits in their heads."

The Goose-girl

————————————————————✳————————————————————

An old queen, whose husband had been dead some years, had a beautiful daughter. When she grew up, she was betrothed to a prince who lived a great way off; and as the time drew near for her to be married, she made ready to set off on her long journey. Her mother, the queen, packed up for her journey many costly things: gold and silver, jewels and trinkets—everything indeed that befitted a royal bride; for she loved her daughter very dearly. To ride with her, and be her companion, and to take care of her, she gave her one of her waiting-maids, charging this woman to bring her in safety into her bridegroom's hands. Now the princess's horse was called Falada, and it could speak.

When the time came for them to set out, the old queen went into the bed-chamber, took a little knife, and cut her finger until the blood came. Three drops only of the blood she let fall upon a handkerchief. This she gave to her daughter, saying, "My child, keep and preserve this with the utmost care; it is a charm that will be of service to you on your way." The princess kissed her mother, and put the precious handkerchief into her bosom.

Early next morning they took a sorrowful leave of one another. The princess mounted her horse and, with her waiting-maid, set off on her journey to her bridegroom's kingdom.

Next day, as they were riding together in the heat and stillness, they came to a little brook; and the princess, being parched with thirst, turned to her maid and said, "I pray thee dismount and fetch me some water in my golden cup out of yonder brook, for I am thirsty and would drink."

"Nay," said the maid insolently, "if you are thirsty, get down yourself and drink as best you can; I don't choose to wait on you any longer."

So thirsty was the princess that she dismounted from her horse, and hastening to the bank of the little brook, knelt down and drank. Frightened at the sullen and angry looks of her waiting-maid, she had not dared to bring with her her golden cup. She was weary, and she wept. "Alas!" she thought to herself, "what will become of me?" And the drops of blood made answer to her and said:

> "*If this your loving mother knew,*
> *Her gentle heart would break in two.*"

But the princess was by nature meek and gentle. She made no complaint, but in silence mounted her horse again.

Thus they continued on their journey; and the sun continued to beat down so scorchingly out of the heavens that the princess began to feel very thirsty again. At last, when after noonday they came to a river, she had forgotten her maid's insolence, and said, "I pray thee dismount, take my golden cup, and fetch me some water from yonder river to drink."

But the maid answered her more rudely and haughtily than before, "Drink if you want to! But fetch your cup yourself. From this time on you get no more of me."

So great was her need that the princess once more dismounted from her horse. She stooped her head over the stream and, having drunken of the running water, sighed deeply and said, "Alas, alas! What will become of me?" And again the three drops of blood made answer and said:

The Goose-girl

"If this your loving mother knew
Her gentle heart would break in two."

Her eyes dim with tears, she stooped lower, and her mother's handkerchief slipped from out of her bosom and floated away with the water. This she had not seen; but her waiting-maid, who sat watching and knew well of this charm, rejoiced. She hated and envied her mistress; and from henceforth she would be in her power.

When, then, the princess arose from her knees and would have mounted her horse again, the maid angrily prevented her. There and then, she compelled her to strip off her bride's apparel and put on her own clothes. Then she mounted Falada, and bade the princess follow her on the jaded nag which she herself had been riding.

The Goose-girl

When, moreover, they were nearing the end of their journey, she drew rein and made the princess swear solemnly by the skies above her that no word of what had passed should ever be uttered to living soul.

"Swear!" she cried, "or you shall pay for it with your life."

In fear and trembling, the princess did as she was bidden; but Falada had seen and heard all this, and had marked it well.

Thus, then, they went on their way until at length they came to the palace of the king. The whole Court rejoiced at their coming. The prince sprang forward to greet them, and lifting the waiting-maid from her horse, supposing her to be the princess who was to be his bride, he led her up the great staircase to the royal chamber. But the princess was bidden to stay in the courtyard below.

Now the old king happened to be looking out of a window, and saw her standing there, and how beautiful she was, and gentle and delicate. And he himself went immediately to the royal guest-chamber, and asked the false princess who it was that she had brought with her and had been left forlornly waiting in the courtyard.

And she lied to the king. "I picked her up on the road," she said, "and brought her with me for company on the long journey. I pray you give the jade some work to do, that she may not be idle."

The old king for some time could not think of any work for the maid to do; but he said at last, "I have a boy who takes care of my geese. She shall help him." Now the name of this boy, who was little more than a child, was Curdken.

That evening the false princess said to the prince, "I beseech you, dear husband, do me one small kindness?"

"That will I," said the prince.

"It is only," she said, "that you send for a slaughterer and tell him to cut off the head of the horse I rode on my journey

hither. It is a stubborn and unruly beast, and plagued me sadly
on the way." This she did because she knew that Falada could
speak, and she feared what secrets he might tell.

The prince listened and said nothing; but a little before dark
set in, the slaughterer did as he had been told. He killed the
princess's horse, Falada, and cut off its head. When the true
princess heard of this, she grieved bitterly and wept; and she
went privily to the slaughterer and promised him a piece of gold
if he would nail up the head of her faithful Falada over the arch
of a great gloomy gateway that led out of the city. There she
would be able to see it every day when she and Curdken went

out in the morning with their geese into the meadows, and came
back at evening. And the slaughterer agreed. He took Falada's
head and that night nailed it fast on the arch above the gloomy
gateway.

Early the next morning, as with their geese she and Curdken
went out through the gate, she looked up at the head nailed
over the dark arch, and said sorrowfully:

> "*Alas, poor Falada, hanging there!*"

And the head made answer:

> "*Alas, poor princess! Ill we fare.*
> *If this your loving mother knew,*
> *Her tender heart would break in two.*"

The two of them went on together out of the city, driving their
geese before them. And when they were come to the meadows,
she sat down upon a green bank and unbound her hair, which

was of pure gold. When Curdken saw it shining and glittering in the sun, he coveted a lock for himself and wanted to pull one out. But she cried:

> *"Blow, blow, blow, sweet wind, I say,*
> *And carry Curdken's hat away;*
> *Let him chase it everywhere—*
> *Hill and dale—and chase in vain,*
> *Till I have combed my golden hair,*
> *And bound its tresses up again."*

And there came a little wind out of the heavens across the meadows. It blew off Curdken's hat, and away it floated and trundled, hill and dale, and away he ran after it. By the time he came back she had finished combing and braiding her golden hair. He was angry and sulked, and refused to speak to her. But they watched and tended their geese until the evening came on, and they drove their flock homeward again.

Next morning, as, with sorrow in her heart, they were passing again under the dark gate, she looked up at the head of her horse, Falada, nailed above the arch, and cried:

> *"Alas, poor Falada, hanging there!"*

And the head answered her:

> *"Alas, poor princess! Ill we fare.*
> *If this your loving mother knew,*
> *Her gentle heart would break in two."*

Then she followed after the geese and so into the meadows; and again began to comb out the tresses of her golden hair. Again Curdken ran up to her, pining to touch it with his hand, and to steal a lock. Again she cried out:

> *"Blow, blow, blow, sweet wind, I say,*
> *And carry Curdken's hat away;*

The Goose-girl

Let him chase it everywhere—
Hill and dale—chase in vain,
Till I have combed my golden hair,
And bound its tresses up again."

Whereupon a gust of wind came out of the cloudless sky; off flew his hat—hill and dale, and far away; and he himself went chasing after it. When he came back, she had done up her hair again, all was safe, and he could steal none of it. In silence they watched and tended their geese until it began to grow dark.

That evening, when they were come back to the palace, Curdken went to the old king, and said, "I refuse to tend the geese with that goose-girl any longer."

"And why?" said the old king.

"She teases and vexes me the whole day long. Besides, she is bewitched."

The old king bade him tell him all that had passed. And Curdken said, "When in the early morning, we go with our geese under the dark gateway out of the city, she begins to weep and wail as we pass a dried-up horse's head that is nailed upon the wall; and she says to it:

'Alas, poor Falada, hanging there!'

"And the head answers:

'Alas, my Princess! Ill we fare.
If this your loving mother knew,
Her tender heart would break in two.' "

He then told the king what happened in the meadows where they kept their geese; how his hat had been blown away, and he had been compelled to chase after it and leave his flock with only the goose-girl to watch over it.

Then the old king bade him drive out his flock of geese as usual the next day. When morning was come, he had concealed himself behind the dark gateway. He watched all that took place, listened closely when the goose-girl spoke to Falada, and marvelled as he heard the head of the dead horse make reply. He then went on himself secretly into the meadows, concealed himself behind the willows at the waterside, and saw with his own eyes how, as soon as she had sat down on the green bank, she unplaited her golden hair, shining and glittering in the sun, and how when Curdken kept on pestering her she cried:

> *"Blow, blow, blow, sweet wind, I say,*
> *And carry Curdken's hat away;*
> *Let him chase it everywhere—*
> *Hill and dale—and chase in vain,*
> *Till I have combed my golden hair,*
> *And bound the tresses up again."*

Yet again the wind blew, and away went the hat and Curdken after it. All this the old king secretly observed. Unseen, he went his way. And when the goose-girl had come home in the evening, he sent for her as he sat alone, and asked her the meaning of these things. And she told the king that she could not reveal her secret, or declare her sorrows to any human being since she had made a vow by the heavens above her never to do so; and that, if she had refused to obey, she would have paid for it by her life. The old king still continued to urge her to share her secret with him, but in vain.

Then said he, "If thou can'st not confide in me, whisper thy sorrows up into the chimney there. It will be well with thee." And he went away. When he had gone, she went to the hearth, as he had counselled her, and began to weep, confessing everything that was in her heart, and saying: "Here am I, utterly alone in the world, and yet the daughter of a king. I have been betrayed by the treachery of a false waiting-maid who has brought me to this woeful pass, and compelled me to put off my royal apparel, and has taken my place with the prince who was to be my bridegroom. Alas, if my mother could see me in these rags, tending the geese, verily her heart would break."

The old king, however, had been listening, and had heard everything that she had said. He returned to her, took her by the hand and kissed her, and bade his servants attire her in raiment befitting a princess. He gazed at her in wonder, marvelling at her beauty. He then sent for his son and told him all that had passed.

The prince rejoiced. No love had sprung up in his heart for the woman who had lied and deceived him. Here at last was the princess, as good as she was beautiful, to whom he had been betrothed.

A great feast was prepared, which was attended by a multitude of the old king's people and many guests. The prince sat at the head of the table, the true princess on the one side of him and the false waiting-maid on the other. But the waiting-maid was so blinded with pride and vanity that she failed to recognize the princess.

When all present had eaten and drunk their fill and were merry, the old king related the whole story. Then he turned to the waiting-maid and put this riddle to her: "What punishment dost thou think should be meted out to any human being guilty of such treachery and wickedness?"

The waiting-maid answered him and said, "She deserves nothing better than to be stripped naked and put into a barrel stuck round with pointed nails. Two white horses should be harnessed to it, to drag her from thy palace through every street of the city, until she is dead."

"Thou art that evil thing," said the king. "As thou hast said, so shall it be done unto thee."

The people rejoiced at the marriage of the prince to his lovely bride; and after the old king's death, they reigned over his kingdom in peace and happiness their whole lives long.

Bash Tshelik—Man of Steel

———————————————————*———————————————————

Long ago in the kingdom of Montenegro the old king was
dying and he summoned his three sons to his bedside. "My
last command to you," he said, to their great amazement,
"is that you must give your sisters in marriage to the very first
suitors who come to ask for their hands. If you do not, may my
eternal curse be upon you." And with those dread words he
turned over and died.

One night, not very long after this, when the royal princesses
(there were three of them) were still going about in their veils of
mourning, there was a tremendous banging at the palace gates
and a ghostly voice was heard to say: "Oh princes, I come to
ask for your eldest sister's hand in marriage." The two eldest
sons said they would refuse to give their sister to an invisible
suitor but the third brother reminded them of their father's
curse and they finally allowed him to lead the princess to the
palace gates.

"May she be a loyal and loving wife to you, whoever you may
be," he said to the invisible suitor, "and may heaven grant that
I may soon see her again." Then, amid the deafening roar of
thunder and blinding flashes of lightning, during which the
whole palace was rocked to its foundations, the princess vanished
with her mysterious bridegroom.

The following night there was another fearful caller at the

palace, this time with a request for the second daughter. Again the two elder brothers would have refused and again the youngest son pleaded and reasoned with them and finally led his second sister out. And again she vanished, too, amid violent peals of thunder and flashes of lightning.

You have probably guessed by now that the same thing happened the next night, too. And you are right. But this time even the youngest son hesitated, for the third princess was his beloved twin sister. At last, however, with his father's threatened curse ringing in his ears, he led her out into the storm, when she, like her two sisters, vanished with no trace.

The three princes now had a long and serious discussion and came to the solemn decision to go out in search of their vanished sisters and not to rest until they had found them. At the end of their first day's travel they decided to pitch their tents by a lake in the middle of a dense forest. As the eldest was taking his turn to keep watch while his brothers slept, he saw an enormous alligator emerge from the middle of the lake and head straight towards him. Undaunted he waited until the monster had reached the edge of the lake and then plunged his sword deep down into its gaping jaws. Then he cut off its scaly ears and placed them in his bag. Not a word of this did he mention to his brothers the next morning and they rode on their way not remotely suspecting how near death they had been.

The end of the second day saw them encamped near a pond in the middle of a marsh. As the second son was keeping guard over his sleeping brothers, an enormous alligator with *two* heads came splashing towards him. With two lightning strokes he severed both heads, cut off the ears and placed them in his bag. Not a word of this did he say to his brothers next morning.

On the night of the third day they arrived at the banks of a large river and the youngest prince took his turn to guard while his brothers slept. From the far side of the river there emerged an alligator with *three* heads and it advanced swiftly to where our young prince was standing. He drew his sword and with a powerful stroke split the three heads in half. He also cut off their ears and placed all six in his bag. However, the powerful splashing of the alligator had entirely quenched the flames of their camp fire and the young prince set off to collect some more dry wood. He had not wandered very far when he espied in the distance nine giants sitting round a fire over which hung a cauldron. Stepping a little nearer he saw to his horror that the cauldron was full of human limbs. Suppressing his fears he walked right up to them and said amiably, "Good evening to you, my friends. I am delighted to have found you at last. I have been searching for you for many years." The giants were equally friendly and invited him to join them in their meal. In the semi-darkness, the prince put on an excellent pretence of eating the human flesh, but in reality he managed to throw every morsel into the bushes behind him.

"Let us now go and hunt for tomorrow's meal," said the giants when they had finished their supper. "The Czar's capital city is full of healthy people who have been providing us with food for many years." Off they went and soon arrived at the city gates. One of the giants uprooted two fir trees and propping one against the wall he told the prince to climb to the top so that they could hand him the second tree, which he would then prop up on the other side of the wall for them to climb down into the city. When he was on top of the wall the prince shouted down to them, "Hi there, I am not quite strong enough to throw down this fir tree alone. Could one of you be so kind as to climb up and help me?" At this one of the giants clambered up and taking hold of the tree as though it were a small twig threw it lightly down over the other side of the wall. But at that very same instant the prince drew his sword, slew the giant and pushed his body over the wall. In the half-darkness those below were quite

unaware of what was going on above their heads. The prince then invited the other eight giants to come up one by one so that he could guide them down over the wall. And as each one arrived at the top, so did our prince slay each one in turn.

The prince himself then climbed down and started to roam through the city streets. But there was hardly a living soul to be seen; either the giants had killed off most of the citizens or the survivors had fled in fear of their lives. Suddenly he espied a light coming from a tall white tower. There were no sentries guarding the gates, so he walked straight in, passing through magnificently furnished halls till he came to a room carpeted and hung entirely with gold. And on a bed in the middle of the room lay the most dazzlingly beautiful girl he had ever seen. But even as he gazed spellbound at her beauty he saw creeping down the wall above her bed a great slimy serpent, its head poised ready to strike. With great presence of mind the young prince hurled his dagger with unerring aim and transfixed the serpent to the wall. And he uttered a prayer: "May Heaven grant that this dagger be not drawn from the wall by any hand save mine." Then he tiptoed silently out of the room, crept out of the tower and made his way out of the deserted city by the same way as he had come. His brothers were still asleep, so he lit a fire, prepared breakfast and woke them up, but not a word did he mention of what had happened during the night.

Now it was the Czar's custom to take a walk round his city each morning to see what new destruction had been committed by the giants. He would be accompanied by one faithful old retainer, one of the very few who had been brave enough to remain in the city, and both together would remove any trace of nightly horror perpetrated by the giants. In this way his beloved daughter, on *her* daily walk, would not meet any mutilated bodies. But on this day, as they approached the city walls, their eyes fell upon the nine dead bodies of the giants. The Czar's joy knew no bounds and on his return to the palace he issued a proclamation announcing a reward of ten thousand ducats to anyone who could give information about their mysterious rescuer. A few moments later his old retainer came in with the news that his daughter had barely escaped death from a vile serpent which had been found transfixed with a dagger to the wall above her bed. The Czar then issued a second proclamation announcing that the unknown hero, if he would make himself known, would receive the hand of the princess in marriage and become heir to the throne.

That same evening the three princes arrived at the Czar's city and stopped to have a meal at the local inn. As a result of the glad news of the death of the giants, the inn was crowded and everyone was drinking and making merry and telling stories.

Bash Tshelik—Man of Steel

The innkeeper invited the young princes to tell of their adventures and each in turn told his story of the horrible alligators. And each one, to prove the truth of his tale, placed the alligator's ears on the table. When the youngest prince threw down six ears there was a gasp of astonishment and admiration and the two elder brothers felt very proud of him.

"But wait," said the young prince, "I haven't finished yet." And he went on to relate his encounter with the giants, his entry into the princess's bedroom and his slaying of the deadly serpent. The innkeeper was so excited that he immediately rushed off to the palace to claim his reward for having found the unknown hero.

The Czar was, of course, overjoyed to hear the news. "Go and bring those princes to the palace at once and you shall have your ten thousand ducats."

The Czar gave a warm welcome to the young men and then proceeded to question the youngest prince about his various exploits.

"Pray tell me, young man," he said, "how you can prove it was you who rescued my daughter."

"If Your Majesty will kindly have me escorted to the princess's bedroom I will show you that I am the only one who can move the dagger from the wall," replied the prince without a trace of boastfulness.

When the Czar saw that this was indeed the case he immediately presented the prince to his daughter as her future bridegroom. The princess was very happy to have such a handsome and heroic young man for her husband and the prince was no less delighted to have such a charming princess for his wife. The wedding was celebrated with great pomp and splendour, after which the two elder brothers resumed their search for their missing sisters.

Although the prince was blissfully happy with his beautiful

bride, however, he, too, after a short while, felt it was his duty to find his sisters, for he missed them very much. The Czar, however, would on no account allow him to leave the country.

One day the Czar was about to set out for an important hunting trip and before leaving he handed the prince a golden ring to which were attached nine small keys. "Eight of these keys," said the Czar, "you may freely use, but this one," he said, pointing to it, "you must on no account ever use, for a terrible disaster would surely occur if you did."

For a day or two the young prince was content to open the eight permitted doors, which were filled with all the priceless treasures of the Czar's realm. But he was itching with curiosity to find out what lay behind the ninth door and on the third day he succumbed to temptation. When he pushed open the door an incredible spectacle met his eyes. An enormous, bearded man, his legs and arms chained in irons, stood in the middle of the room. Around his neck was a heavy thick ring from which four chains led to the four corners of the room. In front of this unfortunate man was a fountain of sparkling water tantalizingly out of reach. "Have pity on me," he moaned to the prince. "Fetch me a cup of water and I will reward you with another life." The prince did so immediately. After gulping this down the man asked imploringly for a second cup. "My name is Bash Tshelik—Man of Steel," he said. "For another cup of water I will give you yet another life." The prince again did as he was requested and was about to go out and lock the door. "Do not leave me yet," pleaded Bash Tshelik, "fetch me one more cup and pour it over my head." The prince did so but no sooner did the water begin to drip down his neck than Bash Tshelik burst his chains, revealing that he also had wings, and rushed from the room. He then burst into the princess's chamber and flew off with her into space.

The Czar returned from his hunt and found his son-in-law broken-hearted and his beloved daughter vanished. Furious though he was with the prince he did not punish him, for he felt he had suffered enough, but he would not on any account permit him to go in search of his wife. "Many of my finest armies were destroyed before Bash Tshelik was finally caught," he said. "If you go after him you will meet with certain death and I could not bear to lose you as well as my daughter." However, the prince was so persistent in his request, refusing either to eat or sleep, that at last the Czar let him go.

After travelling for many weary days the prince came to a dense forest in the midst of which was a castle made entirely of pink transparent marble. He could scarcely believe his eyes when he saw, leaning out of a turret window, none other than his own eldest sister. "Come in, darling brother," she called out joyfully, "but leave your horse tethered in the woods."

Inside the castle the prince was delighted to see his sister looking so happy and well, but he was rather taken aback when he
heard that her husband was the king of the dragons and had
sworn to kill her brothers if they ever dared to venture that way.
"You must hide," she said urgently, "for he will come in at any
moment." When he did arrive the prince saw, through a keyhole, that his brother-in-law took off his dragon's disguise to
reveal himself as a young man of almost godlike beauty. But his
very first words were not very reassuring. "I seem to detect the
odour of human flesh," he remarked. "There is no one here at
all," said his wife, "but supposing one of my brothers were to
visit me, would you really kill him?"

"You know I would slay your two elder brothers," he replied,
"but to your youngest brother I would show the same courtesy
as he showed me when he gave you to me in marriage." The
princess laughed joyously and clapped her hands for her brother
to appear. A great banquet was prepared in his honour, but
when the prince told the story of Bash Tshelik the king pleaded
him to go no further in his quest. "The day you freed him I met
him with ten thousand of my dragons, yet still he escaped, un-
vanquished, after a bloody battle. So how can you fight him
alone?" The prince replied, "I am grateful for your good advice
but I cannot rest until I have found my wife." And he thought
to himself, "I have three lives to gamble with, so what have I to
fear?" The dragon king sadly plucked a feather from his cloak
and presenting it to the prince said, "If ever you need help, burn
this feather and I will come to your help with all my armies."

Setting off once more, the prince, after several days, came to
a castle all of green marble set on the peak of a great mountain.
This time, leaning out of a turret window, his second sister
called out joyfully to him, "Come in, darling brother, and bring
me news of home. But please leave your horse tethered outside."
Once more he was overjoyed to see his sister looking so radiant

and he admired her sumptuous palace and costly robes. "My husband is the king of the eagles," she told him, "and you must hide before he comes in, for he has sworn to kill my brothers." Hidden inside a deep cupboard the prince soon heard the sound of flapping wings and through the keyhole he saw the eagle king taking off his wings and eagle's crest and showing himself to be a most handsome and powerful young man. However, his first words did nothing to reassure the prince. "Is there a stranger somewhere about?" he asked. "Nobody," replied his wife, "but if one of my brothers were to pay a visit how would you treat him?"

"Your two elder brothers I would treat with the utmost severity," came the stern reply, "but to your youngest brother I would show the same courtesy as he showed me that night when he gave you to me in marriage." The princess laughed happily and clapped her hands for her brother to appear. The king celebrated his brother-in-law's visit with a sumptuous feast but when the prince told him the story of Bash Tshelik, the king interrupted him and said earnestly, "Proceed no further in this vain quest. That diabolical monster is invincible and you will meet with certain death."

"Grateful as I am for your kind advice," said the prince, "I cannot rest until I have found my beloved wife."

"Then take this feather," said the eagle king sadly, "and when you find yourself in dire peril burn it and I will come to your aid with all my eagles."

After a few more days' travel the young prince came to a castle of pure white marble standing on the shore of a great lake. In this castle he found his beloved twin sister, now married to the king of the falcons. She told her brother that the falcon king had sworn to take vengeance on her elder brothers but had not forgotten the courtesy he had been shown by her twin brother on that memorable night when he gave her in marriage to him.

Bash Tshelik—Man of Steel

The falcon king, too, tried to dissuade the prince from pursuing Bash Tshelik, but when he saw that nothing would deter him he handed him a feather from his cloak, saying, "When things are desperate, burn this feather and I and all my falcons will come to your aid."

On and on travelled the brave young prince—through forest, mountains and marshland, over barren deserts and precipitous cliffs—until one day he arrived at the entrance to a cave where, cooking a humble meal over a small fire, he saw his own beloved wife. Her lustrous, dark locks hung untidily around her face, her eyes were red with weeping and her dress was torn but she still looked so beautiful that the young prince almost wept at the sight of her. He took her in his arms and all fear of Bash Tshelik seemed to vanish. But his wife begged him with tears in her eyes to leave immediately. "You know how much I would like you to stay, but if that monster returns he will surely slay you," she pleaded. The prince's only reply was swiftly to lift her on to his horse and gallop away. Not many moments elapsed before they heard the frightening beat of wings and Bash Tshelik was upon them. He seized the princess and roared sternly to the prince. "This time I shall pardon you, for I have granted you three lives. But never again must you dare to attempt to recover what I consider to be mine." Whereupon he and the weeping princess disappeared into the clouds.

The daring prince was determined to try his luck once more, remembering that he had two more lives to gamble with. This time he carried off his wife when Bash Tshelik was once more absent and he even managed to get within sight of the Czar's capital. But again the monster caught up with them and again he forgave the prince with a further stern warning.

The prince's third attempt was foiled in the monster's very cave. "You have now forfeited the three lives I granted you," said Bash Tshelik in triumph. "I hope you have more sense than to throw away the life Heaven has granted you." And with that he flung the helpless prince outside the cave.

But the prince did not despair for long. He remembered the three feathers which his brothers-in-law had given him as parting gifts and he decided to make one last attempt to rescue his wife. One morning the princess found him at the door of the cave. Showing her the three feathers and explaining what they meant, he persuaded her to come away with him. Within seconds Bash Tshelik was upon them. Just as the monster was about to shoot one deadly arrow into the prince's heart, the prince took the three feathers from his cap, one by one, and set them alight, and immediately the whole sky was swarming with fire-breathing dragons, masses of eagles holding rocks in their talons, and innumerable falcons all tearing fiercely at Bash Tshelik with their claws. However, although he was scarred and wounded beyond description and blood flowed from him as from a gushing torrent, Bash Tshelik seemed to be invincible, and seizing the princess he fled from the scene of battle back to his lair.

The young prince had been shot and lay as though dead, and his three royal brothers-in-law had to send for healing waters from the holy rivers. The water was brought back in a trice and the prince's wounds healed miraculously as soon as the water touched them. But do you think that he had now given up? Not at all. Despite the advice of the three kings he told them he would never abandon hope as long as there was breath left in his body. The dragon king then gave him this advice: "Go tell your wife to find out by womanly cunning the secret of Bash Tshelik's strength."

The following morning saw the prince arrive steathily at the monster's cave and his wife almost swooned when she saw him, so certain was she that she had left him dead on the battlefield. He told her, when she recovered sufficiently, precisely what questions to ask her captor, and then crept away to a safe hiding-place.

The princess greeted Bash Tshelik with extra-loving warmth when he came back that day. "How strong and powerful you are," she cooed. "I wonder what is the secret of your invincible power."

"Oh weak and foolish woman," replied Bash Tshelik, "my strength lies in my sabre." "But surely", protested the princess softly, winding her white arms about his neck, "you do not rely *only* on your sabre." "Silly creature," laughed the monster, "I have my bow and arrows as well, you know." "I find it so hard to believe, dear Bash Tshelik, that you were able to defeat all those dragons, eagles and falcons simply with your sabre and arrows," said the princess as sweetly as she could. Bash Tshelik was very flattered. "As your husband is no longer alive," he said, "I am able to tell you the whole truth about my secret strength. In the midst of the black mountain which you see not far from our cavern there lives a fox in whose heart is a bird. AND IN THAT BIRD LIES THE SECRET OF MY STRENGTH. But it is well-nigh impossible to catch that wily fox, for it can change itself into every shape and form."

Next morning, when Bash Tshelik had left the cave for his daily hunt, the prince returned stealthily to find out his secret. Then he went straight back to his three royal brothers-in-law and told them the good news. Together they all set out for the black mountain and found the enchanted fox. The eagle king let fly his eagles in hot pursuit but the fox changed itself into a duck and dived into a lake. Whereupon the falcon king set his falcons after it. They chased it high into the clouds, where the dragons soared up after it and finally captured and slew it. Then the prince carefully took out its heart, opened it and found a most monstrous-looking bird inside. He kindled a fire and threw the bird upon it. And at that very instant, just as Bash Tshelik was stepping inside the cave for his midday meal, a dense darkness spread all around him and he fell down dead with a sickening groan that could be heard for miles around. And thus perished the most diabolical of all monsters.

The prince brought his wife home to the Czar's city in great triumph and the following year, when their first baby son was born, his three beloved sisters came to attend the christening, accompanied by their enchanting husbands.

The Nightingale

———————————*———————————

In China, as you know, the Emperor is a Chinaman, and all the folk he has about him are Chinamen too. It's many years ago now, but that is exactly the reason why it is worth while to listen to the story, before it's forgotten. The Emperor's palace was the most splendid in the world, wholly and entirely made of fine porcelain, very costly, but so brittle and risky to touch that one had to take very great care. In the garden the most extraordinary flowers were to be seen, and to the most magnificent of all little silver bells were tied, so that nobody might pass by without noticing the flower. Yes, everything was most carefully thought out in the Emperor's garden, and it extended so far that the gardener himself did not know the end of it. If you went on walking you came into a beautiful forest with tall trees and deep lakes. The forest went right down to the sea, which was blue and deep. Large ships could sail right in beneath the branches, and in the branches there lived a Nightingale, which sang so divinely that even the poor fisherman, who had so much else to think about, stopped and listened when he was out at night pulling up his fishing nets and happened to hear the Nightingale. "Lord, how pretty it is!" he said; but then he had to attend to his business, and forgot the bird. Still, the next night when it sang again, and the fisherman came out here, he said once more: "Lord, how pretty it is!"

From all the countries in the world travellers came to the

The Nightingale

Emperor's city and were amazed at the palace and the garden; but when they came to hear the Nightingale, they all said: "After all, this is the best thing." And the travellers told of it when they got home, and clever people wrote many a book about the City, the Palace and the Garden, but they did not overlook the Nightingale: it was put at the head of everything, and those who could make poetry wrote the loveliest poems all about the Nightingale in the forest by the deep lake.

The books went all over the world, and some of them came, once upon a time, to the Emperor, too. He was sitting in his golden chair reading and reading, and every minute he nodded his head, for it pleased him to hear the splendid description of the City and the Palace and the Garden. "Yet, the Nightingale is the best thing of all," was written there.

"What's this?" said the Emperor. "The Nightingale? Why, I know nothing whatever about it! Is there such a bird in my Empire—not to say in my garden? I never heard of it! This is what one can get by reading."

So he called his Marshal, who was of such high rank that when anyone inferior to him made bold to address him or ask him a question, he never made any reply but "P", which means nothing at all.

"It appears that there is a most remarkable bird here, called a Nightingale," said the Emperor. "It is stated to be the very best thing in my vast realm! Why has no one ever told me anything about it?"

"I have never before heard it spoken of," said the Marshal; "it has never been presented at Court."

"I desire that it shall come here tonight and sing before me," said the Emperor. "Here is the whole world aware of what I possess, and I know nothing of it!"

"I have never before heard it spoken of," said the Marshal; "I must search for it, I must find it."

But where was it to be found? The Marshal ran up and down all the staircases, and through the halls and passages, but no one of all the people he met had heard tell of the Nightingale, and the Marshal ran back to the Emperor and said that it certainly must be an invention of the people who wrote books. "Your Imperial Majesty could never imagine the things people write; all manner of inventions, and something which is called the Black Art."

"But the book in which I read this," said the Emperor, "was sent to me by the high and mighty Emperor of Japan, so it cannot be an untruth. I *will* hear the Nightingale! It must be here tonight. It has my most exalted favour, and if it does not come, the whole court shall have its stomachs stamped upon, when it has dined!"

"Tsing-pe!" said the Marshal; and ran again up and down all the staircases and through all the halls and passages; and half the court ran with him, for they did not at all wish to have their stomachs stamped upon. There was ever such a hue and cry after this remarkable Nightingale, which was known to the whole world, but to nobody at the court.

At last they came on a poor little girl in the kitchen. She said: "O Lord, the Nightingale? I know it well; yes, indeed, how it can sing! Every evening I have leave to carry home leavings from the table to my poor sick mother. She lives down by the shore, and when I'm coming back and am tired and take a rest in the wood, I hear the Nightingale sing. The tears come in my eyes with it: it feels as if my mother was kissing me."

"Little kitchen girl," said the Marshal, "I will promise you a permanent position in the kitchen and leave to see the Emperor dine, if you can guide us to the Nightingale, for it is invited for this evening." So they all set out together for the wood where the Nightingale used to sing. Half the court was there. As they were making the best of their way along, a cow began to low.

The Nightingale

"Oh!" said the court pages. "Now we can hear it; it's a really remarkable power for such a small animal! I'm quite sure I've heard it before."

"No, that's the cow lowing," said the little kitchen girl. "We're a long way off the place yet."

Then the frogs began croaking in the pond.

"Lovely," said the Chinese master of the palace. "Now I hear her! It resembles small church bells."

"No, that's the frogs," said the little kitchen girl; "but I think we shall hear it very soon now."

Then the Nightingale began to sing.

"That's it," said the little girl. "Hark! hark! And there it sits!" And she pointed to a little grey bird up among the branches. "Is it possible?" said the Marshal. "I could never have imagined it would be like that! And how shabby it looks! It must certainly have lost its colour at the sight of so many distinguished persons in its vicinity."

"Little Nightingale," the little kitchen girl called out aloud; "our gracious Emperor very much wants you to sing to him."

"With the greatest of pleasure," said the Nightingale, and sang so that it was a pure delight.

"It resembles glass bells," said the Marshal, "and look at its little throat, how it works it! It is most curious that we should never have heard it before! It will have a great success at court." "Shall I sing once again for the Emperor?" said the Nightingale, who thought the Emperor was there too.

"My excellent little Nightingale," said the Marshal, "I have the great pleasure of being commanded to invite you to a court festival this evening, where you will enchant his exalted Imperial Grace with your charming song."

"It sounds best out in the green wood," said the Nightingale. But it gladly accompanied them when it heard that the Emperor asked for it.

At the palace there was a tremendous smartening up. The walls and floors, which were of porcelain, shone with the light of many thousands of golden lamps. The most beautiful flowers, which really could ring, were set about the windows. There was a running to and fro, and a draught of air, but that made all the bells ring till one couldn't hear one's own voice.

In the middle of the great hall where the Emperor sat, a golden perch was set up, and on it the Nightingale was to sit. The whole court was there, and the little kitchen girl had got

permission to stand behind the door, seeing now she had the
title of Actual Kitchen-maid. Everybody was in their best attire,
and everybody was looking at the little grey bird. The Emperor
nodded to it.

And the Nightingale sang so beautifully that tears came into
the eyes of the Emperor; the tears ran down his cheeks, and then
the Nightingale sang yet more delightfully, so that it went
straight to his heart; and the Emperor was greatly pleased, and
said that the Nightingale should have his golden slipper to wear
on its neck. But the Nightingale thanked him and said it had
already had reward enough.

"I have seen tears in the Emperor's eyes; that is to me the
richest of treasures. An Emperor's tears have a marvellous
power. God knows I am well paid." And it sang again with that
sweet divine voice.

"It is the most lovable coquetterie one can conceive," said the whole suite of ladies, and they put water in their mouths so as to gurgle when anyone spoke to them; they thought that they too were Nightingales. Yes, and the lackeys and chamber-maids let it be understood that they also were satisfied, and that means a lot, for they are the most difficult people to suit. In fact, the Nightingale really did make a great success.

It was now to remain at court and have its own cage, and liberty to take exercise out of doors twice in the day time and once at night. It had twelve attendants, each of whom had a silken thread attached to its leg, which they held tight. There really was no satisfaction in these expeditions. The whole City talked of the remarkable bird, and when two people met, one of them would say nothing but "night" and the other would say "gale". Whereupon they heaved a sigh and understood each other. Nay, more than eleven pork butchers' children were named after it, but not one of them had a note of music in its body.

One day there arrived a large parcel for the Emperor; on it was written, "Nightingale".

"Here now we have another book about our celebrated bird," said the Emperor; but it was not a book, it was a little machine, that lay in a box—an artificial Nightingale made to resemble the live one, but all set with diamonds, rubies and sapphires. As soon as ever the artificial bird was wound up, it could sing one of the strains the real one sang, and its tail moved up and down and glistened with silver and gold. Round its neck hung a little ribbon, and on it was written: "The Emperor of Japan's Nightingale is poor beside that of the Emperor of China."

"That is charming!" said everybody. And the man who had brought the artificial bird immediately received the title of Chief Imperial Bringer of Nightingales.

Now they must sing together; what a duet it will be!

So they had to sing together; but it wouldn't go right, for the

real Nightingale sang in its own style, and the artificial bird
went off into waltz-tunes.

"No blame attaches to it," said the bandmaster; "it keeps
excellent time, and is entirely of my school." So the artificial
bird was to sing alone. It made as great a success as the real one,
and was, besides, far prettier to look at; it glittered like a brace-
let or a brooch.

Three-and-thirty times over did it sing the self-same melody,
and yet it was not tired. The people would have liked to hear it
over again, but the Emperor said that now the live Nightingale
should sing a little—but where was it? Nobody had noticed that
it had flown out of the open window, away to its own green
wood.

"But what is the meaning of this?" said the Emperor. And all
the court people scolded, and said the Nightingale was a most
ungrateful creature. "Still, we have the best bird, after all," they

said; and the artificial bird had to sing again. It was the thirty-fourth time they had heard the same piece, but they didn't quite know it yet, for it was very difficult, and the bandmaster praised the bird in the highest terms, and assured them that it was superior to the real Nightingale, not only as regards the plumage and the many beautiful diamonds, but also internally.

"For observe, your lordships, and the Emperor above all, with the real Nightingale one can never calculate what will come next, but with the artificial bird all is definite; it is thus, and not otherwise. It can be accounted for; one can open it up and show the human contrivance, how the waltzes are set, how they go, and how one follows on another."

"Exactly what I think," said everybody; and the bandmaster got permission on the following Sunday to exhibit the bird to the people. They too should hear it sing, said the Emperor. And they did hear it, and were as delighted as if they had got drunk on tea (which is the genuine Chinese fashion), and everyone said "oh" and pointed the finger we call lick-pot up in the air and then nodded. But the poor fisherman, who had heard the real Nightingale, said: "It sings pretty enough, and it's like it too; but there's something wanting, I don't know what!"

The real Nightingale was exiled from the land and realm. The artificial bird had a place assigned it on a silk cushion close to the Emperor's bed. All the presents that had been made to it, gold and jewels, lay round it, and it had risen to the title of "High Imperial Nightingale Songster" and in precedence was Number One on the Left Hand Side; for the Emperor accounted that side to be the most distinguished on which the heart lay, and even an Emperor's heart is on the left side. And the bandmaster wrote five-and-twenty volumes on the subject of the artificial bird. The work was very learned and very long, full of the most difficult words in the Chinese language, and everyone said they had read it and understood it; for otherwise they would have been accounted stupid and would have had their stomachs stamped upon.

So things went on for a whole year. The Emperor, the court, and all the rest of the Chinese knew by heart every little cluck in the artificial bird's song, but precisely for that reason they liked it all the better: they could sing with it themselves, and so they did. The street boys would sing "Zizizi! kluk, kluk, kluk!" and the Emperor sang too: in fact, it was admittedly exquisite.

But one evening, when the bird was singing its best and the Emperor was lying in bed listening to it, something went "snap" inside the bird. Whirr-rr! All the wheels whizzed round, and the music stopped. The Emperor jumped straight out of bed, and had his body physician summoned, but what use was that? They fetched the watchmaker, and after much talk and much examination, he got the bird into order after a fashion. But he said it must be most sparingly used, for it was very much worn in the bearings, and it was impossible to replace them so that you could be sure of the music. That was a sad affliction! Only once a year durst they let the bird sing, and even that was a severe strain. But thereupon the bandmaster made a short oration with plenty of difficult words, and said that it was just as good as before, and accordingly it was just as good as before.

Five years had now passed by and a really great sorrow came upon the whole country, for at bottom they were very fond of their Emperor, and now he was ill, and it was said, could not recover. A new Emperor was now chosen, and people stood outside in the streets and asked the Marshal how it went with their Emperor.

"P," said he, and shook his head.

Cold and pale lay the Emperor in his great stately bed; the whole court believed him dead, and every one of them ran off to pay their respects to the new Emperor. The servants of the bed-chamber ran out to gossip about it, and the palace maids had a large coffee party. Everywhere in all the halls and corridors, cloth was laid down so that footsteps should not be heard, and so everything was very, very quiet. But the Emperor was not yet dead; stiff and pale he lay there in the stately bed with the long velvet curtains and the heavy gold tassels: high up a window stood open, and the moon shone in upon the Emperor and the artificial bird.

The poor Emperor was hardly able to draw his breath; it seemed as if something was sitting on his chest. He opened his eyes, and then he saw that it was Death, who was sitting on his breast, and had put on his golden crown, and was holding in one hand the gold sword of the Emperor, and in the other his splendid banner: and round about, in the folds of the great velvet bed curtains, strange faces pushed themselves out, some quite horrible, others divinely kind. There were all the Emperor's good and evil deeds, looking at him now that Death was seated upon his breast.

"Do you remember that?" whispered one after another. "Do you remember that?" And they told him of many things, so that the sweat broke out on his forehead. "I never knew of that," said the Emperor. "Music! Music! The great drum of China!" he called out, "that I may not hear all they are saying."

They went on, and Death nodded like a Chinaman at everything that was said.

"Music! Let me have music!" cried the Emperor. "You blessed little bird of gold, sing, do sing! I have given you gold and precious things; I myself hung my golden slipper about your neck! Sing, do sing!"

But the bird was silent: there was no one to wind it up, and without that it did not sing. But Death went on looking at the Emperor out of his great empty eye-holes, and everything was still, fearfully still.

At that instant there was heard close by the window, the most lovely song. It was the little Nightingale that was sitting on the branch outside. It had heard the Emperor's need, and so had come to sing to him of comfort and hope: and as it sung, the forms became more and more shadowy. The blood coursed quicker and quicker through the Emperor's weak body, and Death himself listened and said: "Go on, little Nightingale! Go on."

"Yes, if you will give me the splendid gold sword! Yes, if you will give me the rich banner, and give me the Emperor's crown." And Death gave each of the treasures for a song, and the Nightingale still went on singing; and it sang of the quiet churchyard and where the white roses grow, where the elder tree smells sweet, and where the fresh grass is moistened with the tears of those who are left. Then a yearning for his garden came upon Death, and he floated out of the window like a cold white mist.

"Thanks, thanks," said the Emperor, "you heavenly little bird, I know you now. I drove you out of my land and realm, and yet you have sung the foul sins away from my bed, and rid my heart of Death. How shall I repay you?"

"You have repaid me," said the Nightingale. "I drew tears from your eyes the first time I sang, and I shall never forget it to you. Those are the jewels that do the heart of the singer good. But sleep now, and become well and strong. I will sing to you."

And it sang, and the Emperor fell into a sweet sleep, a sleep that was kind and healing.

The sun was shining in at the windows on him when he awoke, strengthened and whole. None of his attendants had come back yet, for they believed he was dead, but the Nightingale still sat there singing.

"You must always stay with me," said the Emperor. "You shall only sing when you like, and as for the artificial bird, I'll break it into a thousand bits."

"Don't do that," said the Nightingale; "it has done what good it could, keep it as before. I can't make any home at the palace, but do let me come here when I like. Then I will sit at evening time on a branch there by this window and sing to you, to make you happy, and thoughtful too. I will sing about the happy and about those who suffer. I will sing of the evil and the good that is about you and is hidden from you. The little singing bird flies far and wide, to the poor fisherman, to the labourer's cottages, to everyone who is far removed from you and your court. I love your heart better than your crown; and yet the crown has about it a perfume of something holy. I will come, I will sing to you; but one thing you must promise me."

"Anything," said the Emperor, as he stood there in his imperial robes, which he had put on himself, and held the sword, heavy with gold, up against his heart.

"One thing I beg of you. Tell no one that you have a little bird that tells you everything. It will be better." And with that the Nightingale flew away.

The attendants came in to see their dead Emperor, and—well, there stood they, and the Emperor said: "Good morning."

The Magic Fishbone

———————————————*———————————————

There was once a King, and he had a Queen, and he was
the manliest of his sex, and she was the loveliest of hers.
The King was, in his private profession, under Govern-
ment. The Queen's father had been a medical man out of
town.

They had nineteen children, and were always having more.
Seventeen of these children took care of the baby, and Alicia,
the eldest, took care of them all. Their ages varied from seven
years down to seven months.

Let us now resume our story.

One day the King was going to the office when he stopped at
the fishmonger's to buy a pound and a half of salmon not too
near the tail, which the Queen (who was a careful housekeeper)
had requested him to send home. Mr. Pickles, the fishmonger,
said, "Certainly, sir, is there any other article? Good morning."

The King went on towards the office in a melancholy mood,
for quarter day was such a long way off and several of the dear
children were growing out of their clothes. He had not proceeded far when Mr. Pickles's errand boy came running after
him and said, "Sir, you didn't notice the old lady in our shop."

"What old lady?" inquired the King. "I saw none."

Now, the King had not seen any old lady because this old
lady had been invisible to him, though visible to Mr. Pickles's

boy. Probably because he messed and splashed the water about
to that degree, and flopped the pairs of soles down in that violent
manner, that, if she had not been visible to him, he would have
spoiled her clothes.

Just then the old lady came trotting up. She was dressed in
shot silk of the richest quality, smelling of dried lavender.

"King Watkins the First, I believe?" said the old lady.

"Watkins," replied the King, "is my name."

"Papa, if I am not mistaken, of the beautiful Princess Alicia?"
said the old lady.

"And eighteen other darlings," replied the King.

"Listen. You are going to the office," said the old lady.

It instantly flashed upon the King that she must be a fairy, or how could she know that?

"You are right," said the old lady, answering his thoughts, "I am the good fairy Grandmarina. Attend. When you return home to dinner, politely invite the Princess Alicia to have some of the salmon you bought just now."

"It may disagree with her," said the King.

The old lady became so very angry at this absurd idea that the King was quite alarmed and humbly begged her pardon.

"We hear a great deal too much about this thing disagreeing and that thing disagreeing," said the old lady with the greatest contempt it was possible to express. "Don't be greedy. I think you want it all yourself."

The King hung his head under this reproof and said he wouldn't talk about things disagreeing any more.

"Be good, then," said the fairy Grandmarina, "and don't! When the beautiful Princess Alicia consents to partake of the salmon—as I think she will—you will find she will leave a fishbone on her plate. Tell her to dry it, and to rub it, and to polish it till it shines like mother-of-pearl, and to take care of it as a present from me."

"Is that all?" asked the King.

"Don't be impatient, sir," returned the fairy Grandmarina, scolding him severely. "Don't catch people short before they have done speaking. Just the way with you grown-up persons. You are always doing it."

The King again hung his head and said he wouldn't do so any more.

"Be good, then," said the fairy Grandmarina, "and don't! Tell the Princess Alicia, with my love, that the fishbone is a magic present which can only be used once; but that it will bring her, that once, whatever she wishes for, PROVIDED SHE

WISHES FOR IT AT THE RIGHT TIME. That is the message. Take care of it."

The King was beginning, "Might I ask the reason——?" when the fairy became absolutely furious.

"Will you be good, sir?" she exclaimed, stamping her foot on the ground. "The reason for this, and the reason for that, indeed! You are always wanting the reason. No reason. There! Hoity toity me! I am sick of your grown-up reasons."

The King was extremely frightened by the old lady's flying into such a passion, and said he was very sorry to have offended her and he wouldn't ask for reasons any more.

"Be good, then," said the old lady, "and don't!"

With those words Grandmarina vanished, and the King went on and on and on till he came to the office. There he wrote and wrote and wrote till it was time to go home again. Then he politely invited the Princess Alicia, as the fairy had directed him, to partake of the salmon. And when she had enjoyed it very much, he saw the fishbone on her plate, as the fairy had told him he would, and he delivered the fairy's message, and the Princess Alicia took care to dry the bone, and to rub it, and to polish it till it shone like mother-of-pearl.

And so when the Queen was going to get up in the morning, she said: "Oh, dear me, dear me, my head, my head!" And then she fainted away.

The Princess Alicia, who happened to be looking in at the chamber door, asking about breakfast, was very much alarmed when she saw her royal mamma in this state, and she rang the bell for Peggy—which was the name of the Lord Chamberlain. But remembering where the smelling bottle was, she climbed on a chair and got it, and after that she climbed on another chair by the bedside and held the smelling bottle to the Queen's nose, and after that she climbed down and got some water, and after that she jumped up again and wetted the Queen's forehead, and, in short, when the Lord Chamberlain came in, that dear old woman said to the little Princess: "What a Trot you are! I couldn't have done it better myself!"

But that was not the worst of the good Queen's illness. Oh, no! She was very ill indeed, for a long time. The Princess Alicia kept the seventeen young Princes and Princesses quiet, and dressed and undressed and danced the baby, and made the kettle boil, and heated the soup, and swept the hearth, and poured out the medicine, and nursed the Queen, and did all that ever she could, and was busy, busy, busy, as busy could be. For there were not many servants at that palace, for three reasons: because the King was short of money, because a rise in his office never seemed to come, and because quarter day was so far off that it looked almost as far off and as little as one of the stars.

But on the morning when the Queen fainted away, where was the magic fishbone? Why, there it was in the Princess Alicia's pocket. She had almost taken it out to bring the Queen to life again when she put it back and looked for the smelling bottle.

After the Queen had come out of her swoon that morning, and was dozing, the Princess Alicia hurried upstairs to tell a most particular secret to a most particularly confidential friend of hers, who was a Duchess. People did suppose her to be a doll but she was really a Duchess, though nobody knew it except the Princess.

This most particular secret was a secret about the magic fishbone, the history of which was well known to the Duchess because the Princess told her everything. The Princess knelt down by the bed on which the Duchess was lying, fully dressed and wide awake, and whispered the secret to her. The Duchess smiled and nodded. People might have supposed that she never smiled and nodded, but she often did, though nobody knew it except the Princess.

Then the Princess Alicia hurried downstairs again to keep

watch in the Queen's room. She often kept watch by herself in the Queen's room; but every evening, while the illness lasted, she sat there watching with the King. And every evening the King sat looking at her with a cross look, wondering why she never brought out the magic fishbone. As often as she noticed this, she ran upstairs, whispered the secret to the Duchess over again and said to the Duchess besides: "They think we children never have a reason or a meaning!" And the Duchess, though the most fashionable Duchess that ever was heard of, winked her eye.

"Alicia," said the King one evening when she wished him good night.

"Yes, Papa."

"What is become of the magic fishbone?"

"In my pocket, Papa."

"I thought you had lost it."

"Oh, no, Papa!"

"Or forgotten it."

"No, indeed, Papa."

And so another time the dreadful little snapping pug dog next door made a rush at one of the young Princes as he stood on the steps coming home from school and terrified him out of his wits, and he put his hand through a pane of glass and bled bled bled. When the seventeen other young Princes and Princesses saw him bleed bleed bleed, they were terrified out of their wits, too, and screamed themselves black in their seventeen faces all at once. But the Princess put her hands over all their seventeen mouths, one after another, and persuaded them to be quiet because of the sick Queen. And then she put the Prince's wounded hand in a basin of fresh cold water, while they stared with their twice seventeen are thirty-four put down four and carry three eyes, and then she looked in the hand for bits of glass and there were fortunately no bits of glass there. And then she said to chubby-legged Princes, who were sturdy, though small: "Bring me in the Royal rag bag. I must snip and stitch and cut and contrive." So those two young Princes tugged at the Royal rag bag and lugged it in, and the Princess Alicia sat down on the floor with a large pair of scissors and a needle and thread, and snipped and stitched and cut and contrived, and made a bandage and put it on, and it fitted beautifully, and so when it was all done she saw the King her papa looking on by the door.

"Alicia."

"Yes, Papa."

"What have you been doing?"

"Snipping, stitching, cutting and contriving, Papa."

"Where is the magic fishbone?"

"In my pocket, Papa."

"I thought you had lost it."

"Oh, no, Papa."

"Or forgotten it."

"No, indeed, Papa."

After that she ran upstairs to the Duchess and told her what had passed, and told her the secret over again, and the Duchess shook her flaxen curls and laughed with her rosy lips.

The Magic Fishbone

Well! and so another time the baby fell under the grate. The seventeen young Princes and Princesses were used to it, for they were always falling under the grate or down the stairs, but the baby was not used to it yet, and it gave him a swelled face and a black eye. The way the poor little darling came to tumble was that he slid out of the Princess Alicia's lap just as she was sitting in a great coarse apron that quite smothered her, in front of the kitchen fire, beginning to peel the turnips for the broth for dinner; and the way she came to be doing that was that the King's cook had run away that morning with her own true love, who was a very tall but very tipsy soldier. Then the seventeen young Princes and Princesses, who cried at everything that happened, cried and roared. But the Princess Alicia (who couldn't help crying a little herself) quietly called to them to be still on account of not throwing back the Queen upstairs, who was fast getting well, and said: "Hold your tongues, you wicked little monkeys, every one of you, while I examine the baby!" Then she examined Baby, and found that he hadn't broken anything, and she held cold iron to his poor dear eye and smoothed his poor dear face, and he presently fell asleep in her arms. Then she said to the seventeen Princes and Princesses: "I am afraid to lay him down yet, lest he should wake and feel pain. Be good and you shall all be cooks." They jumped for joy when they heard that, and began making themselves cooks' caps out of old newspapers. So to one she gave the salt box, and to one she gave the barley, and to one she gave the herbs, and to one she gave the turnips, and to one she gave the carrots, and to one she gave the onions, and to one she gave the spice box, till they were all cooks and all running about at work, she sitting in the middle smothered in the great coarse apron, nursing Baby. By and by the broth was done, and the baby woke up smiling like an angel, and was trusted to the sedatest Princess to hold, while the other Princes and Princesses were squeezed into a far-off corner to look at the Princess Alicia turning out the saucepanful of broth, for fear (as they were always getting into trouble) they should get splashed and scalded. When the broth came tumbling out,

steaming beautifully and smelling like a nosegay good to eat, they clapped their hands. That made the baby clap his hands, and that, and his looking as if he had a comic toothache, made all the Princes and Princesses laugh. So the Princess Alicia said: "Laugh and be good, and after dinner we will make him a nest on the floor in a corner, and he shall sit in his nest and see a dance of eighteen cooks." That delighted the young Princes and Princesses, and they ate up all the broth, and washed up all the plates and dishes and cleared away, and pushed the table into a corner, and then they, in their cooks' caps, and the Princess Alicia in the smothering coarse apron that belonged to the cook that had run away with her own true love that was the very tall but very tipsy soldier, danced a dance of eighteen cooks before the angelic baby, who forgot his swelled face and his black eye and crowed with joy.

And so then, once more the Princess Alicia saw King Watkins the First, her father, standing in the doorway looking on, and he said:

"What have you been doing, Alicia?"

"Cooking and contriving, Papa."

"What else have you been doing, Alicia?"

"Keeping the children light-hearted, Papa."

"Where is the magic fishbone, Alicia?"

"In my pocket, Papa."

"I thought you had lost it."

"Oh, no, Papa."

"Or forgotten it."

"No, indeed, Papa."

The King then sighed so heavily and seemed so low-spirited and sat down so miserably, leaning his head upon his hand and his elbow upon the kitchen table pushed away in the corner, that the seventeen Princes and Princesses crept softly out of the kitchen and left him alone with the Princess Alicia and the angelic baby.

"What is the matter, Papa?"

"I am dreadfully poor, my child."

156

"Have you no money at all, Papa?"

"None, my child."

"Is there no way left of getting any, Papa?"

"No way," said the King. "I have tried very hard, and I have tried all ways."

When she heard those last words, the Princess Alicia began to put her hand into the pocket where she kept the magic fishbone.

"Papa," said she, "when we have tried very hard and tried all ways, we must have done our very, very best?"

"No doubt, Alicia."

"When we have done our very, very best, Papa, and that is not enough, then I think the right time must have come for asking help of others." This was the very secret connected with the magic fishbone which she had found out for herself from the good fairy Grandmarina's words, and which she had so often whispered to her beautiful and fashionable friend the Duchess.

So she took out of her pocket the magic fishbone that had been dried and rubbed and polished till it shone like mother-of-pearl, and she gave it one little kiss and wished it was quarter day. And immediately it was quarter day, and the King's quarter's salary came rattling down the chimney and bounced into the middle of the floor.

But this was not half of what happened, no, not a quarter, for immediately afterwards the good fairy Grandmarina came riding in in a carriage and four peacocks, with Mr. Pickles's boy up behind, dressed in silver and gold, with a cocked hat, powdered hair, pink silk stockings, a jewelled cane and a nosegay. Down jumped Mr. Pickles's boy with his cocked hat in his hand and wonderfully polite (being entirely changed by enchantment) and handed Grandmarina out, and there she stood in her rich shot silk smelling of dried lavender, fanning herself with a sparkling fan.

"Alicia, my dear," said this charming old fairy, "how do you do, I hope I see you pretty well, give me a kiss."

The Princess Alicia embraced her, and then Grandmarina turned to the King and said rather sharply: "Are you good?"

The King said he hoped so.

"I suppose you know the reason now why my god-daughter here," kissing the Princess again, "did not apply to the fishbone sooner?" said the fairy.

The King made her a shy bow.

"Ah! But you didn't then!" said the fairy.

The King made her a shyer bow.

"Any more reasons to ask for?" said the fairy.

The King said no, and he was very sorry.

"Be good, then," said the fairy, "and live happy ever afterwards."

Then Grandmarina waved her fan, and the Queen came in most splendidly dressed, and the seventeen young Princes and Princesses, no longer grown out of their clothes, came in newly fitted out from top to toe, with tucks in everything to admit of its being let out. After that the fairy tapped the Princess Alicia with her fan, and the smothering coarse apron flew away, and she appeared exquisitely dressed like a little bride, with a wreath of orange flowers and a silver veil. After that the kitchen dresser changed of itself into a wardrobe, made of beautiful woods and gold and looking-glass, which was full of dresses of all sorts, all for her and all exactly fitting her. After that the angelic baby came in, running alone, with his face and eye not a bit the worse but much the better. Then Grandmarina begged to be introduced to the Duchess, and when the Duchess was brought down many compliments passed between them.

A little whispering took place between the fairy and the Duchess, and then the fairy said out loud: "Yes, I thought she would have told you." Grandmarina then turned to the King and Queen and said: "We are going in search of Prince Certainpersonio. The pleasure of your company is requested at church in half an hour precisely." So she and the Princess Alicia got into the carriage, and Mr. Pickles's boy handed in the Duchess, who sat by herself on the opposite seat, and then Mr. Pickles's boy put up the steps and got up behind, and the peacocks flew away with their tails spread.

Prince Certainpersonio was sitting by himself, eating barley sugar and waiting to be ninety. When he saw the peacocks followed by the carriage coming in at the window, it immediately occurred to him that something uncommon was going to happen.

"Prince," said Grandmarina, "I bring you your bride."

The moment the fairy said those words, Prince Certainpersonio's face left off being sticky, and his jacket and corduroys changed to peach-bloom velvet, and his hair curled, and a cap and feather flew in like a bird and settled on his head. He got into the carriage by the fairy's invitation, and there he renewed his acquaintance with the Duchess, whom he had seen before.

In the church were the Prince's relations and friends, and the Princess Alicia's relations and friends, and the seventeen Princes and Princesses, and the baby, and a crowd of neighbours. The marriage was beautiful beyond expression. The Duchess was bridesmaid and beheld the ceremony from the pulpit, where she was supported by the cushion of the desk.

Grandmarina gave a magnificent wedding feast afterwards, in which there was everything and more to eat, and everything and more to drink. The wedding cake was delicately ornamented with white satin ribbons, frosted silver and white lilies, and was forty-two yards around.

When Grandmarina had drunk her love to the young couple, and Prince Certainpersonio had made a speech, and everybody cried Hip, Hip, Hip Hurrah! Grandmarina announced to the King and Queen that in the future there would be eight quarter days in every year, except in leap year, when there would be ten. She turned to Certainpersonio and Alicia and said: "My dears, you will have thirty-five children, and they will all be good and beautiful. Seventeen of your children will be boys, and eighteen will be girls. The hair of your children will curl naturally. They will never have the measles and will have recovered from the whooping cough before being born.

"It only remains," said Grandmarina, "to make an end of the fishbone."

So she took it from the hand of the Princess Alicia, and it instantly flew down the throat of the dreadful little snapping pug dog next door and choked him, and he expired in convulsions.

Gawaine and the Green Knight

---------------------------------*---------------------------------

King Arthur and his court had been keeping Christmas at Camelot with joyful feasting and merrymaking, and now was New Year's Day come with gifts and games and much festivity, and a great banquet to crown all. Outside the snow lay white and glittering and a cold wind blew, but in the great hall of the castle all was warm and gay, with huge fires burning on the hearthstones and bright colours everywhere.

Just as the merry company was sitting down to feast, the high doors of the hall blew open and in from the snow there rode a warrior, so tall that he might almost have been called a giant.

Everyone fell silent in astonishment, for the face and the hands of this stranger and all that might be seen of his body were as green as the Maytime grass, and his long green hair and his green beard were cut evenly around him at the level of his elbows, so that they hung like a short cape about him. His jerkin, his hose, and his mantle were green, all embroidered with birds and butterflies in gold. His horse, too, was green and a mighty creature, well fitted to carry such a huge man, with its trappings all of green leather studded with emeralds, and its green mane and tail plaited and entwined with golden ribbons, and little golden bells hanging tinkling from its forelock. In one hand the stranger carried a branch of holly, and in the other a great battle-axe with a green haft and a blade of green steel.

Gawaine and the Green Knight

This Green Knight rode up the length of the hall and then called out, "Where is the master of this house?"

And Arthur stood up and answered him, bidding him welcome. "Dismount and eat with us, for this is the feast of the New Year, and all guests are gladly received."

"I have not come to feast with you," replied the Green Knight.

"This is a season of goodwill," said Arthur. "May God grant you come in peace."

"At home," answered the Green Knight, "I have armour and a helmet, a shield and a sharp sword, and many other weapons. Think you that if I had meant to give battle to any man I would have ridden forth unarmed? No, my lord King Arthur, I have come in peace. Because I have heard great talk of the courage and prowess of your knights, I have come to find if there is any here will join with me in a sport I have devised."

"If you would meet one of my knights in combat," said Arthur, "I have no doubt that there will be several here who will give you the sport you ask."

The Green Knight shook his head. "It is not fighting that I seek. It is no more than a Christmas game to bring mirth to your feasting." He held up the green axe which he carried. "If there is any bold man here who would win this axe for his own, let him come and take it, and with it give me one blow, and pledge me his word that when a year is past from today, he will seek me out and take in return one blow from me."

At first all were too amazed to answer him; and then from where he sat beside Queen Guenever young Sir Gawaine, King Arthur's nephew, spoke. "If you will give me leave, my lord King, I will accept this challenge."

When Arthur had given his consent, Gawaine rose and went to the Green Knight and took the axe from him. The Green Knight dismounted and looked steadily at Gawaine. "Tell me your name," he said, "and give me your word to seek me out and take a blow from me, a year from today."

"My name is Gawaine, and you have my word for it, sir green stranger. But where shall I find you, when a year is past?"

The Green Knight laughed. "That must you discover for yourself. Now give me a blow. Just one, no more." And he bent his head for the stroke.

Gawaine stood firmly and raised the great axe and swung it downward upon the Green Knight's neck with such strength and skill that the green head was severed from the body and rolled among the rushes on the floor, and a cry of admiration for the blow rose up from all those gathered there.

"He has indeed found the game he asked for, the green stranger," laughed Sir Kay the Seneschal.

Yet the admiration was turned to amazement when they saw how the Green Knight neither fell nor even staggered, but instead bent down and picked up his green head by the hair. He went to his horse, set his foot firmly in the stirrup, and mounted. Then he held up his head high before them, and the lips parted and the head spoke to Sir Gawaine. "Forget not to come and seek me, a year from today, to take the blow that I have promised you." And with that the Green Knight, still carrying his head, rode out from the hall into the snow.

For all the rest of that day the company could talk of nothing else save the Green Knight and his head; and his axe was set up on the wall for all to marvel at. And Gawaine made light of the matter and laughed, and called it a rare Christmas jest.

But as the year grew older and summer followed spring, Sir Gawaine began to consider it less of a jest. And when the red and yellow leaves and the golden moon of Michaelmas were come, he went to Arthur and said, "It is time for me to ride forth and seek the Green Knight, for I know not where he is to be found nor how long it will be before I find him, and I would not be late at our tryst. Give me your leave to depart."

So Gawaine rode forth on Gringolet his horse, all shining in gold and scarlet and well armed. He wandered through the whole land, alone, without even a squire to serve him, and in every place he asked if any man had heard of a green knight who rode upon a green horse, but no one could answer him. And the winter came upon him as he travelled, with icy wind and snow, but never a word did he hear of his quest.

At last, on Christmas Eve, he came upon a castle and asked shelter for the night. The lord of the castle and his lady received him gladly, and bade him spend the days of Christmas feasting in their company. The lord was a tall strong man with red hair and beard, and his lady was, so Gawaine thought, the fairest he had ever seen until that moment; and they both gave him such a welcome that he forgot for a while the perils of his quest.

When the three days of the festival were done, the lord of the castle asked Gawaine, "What brings you so far from King Arthur's court in the winter-time, when ways are hard?"

And Gawaine told him of the Green Knight and how he must find him, and he sighed and said, "Tomorrow I must leave you, for there is but little time left to me, if I would be with the Green Knight on New Year's Day."

The lord of the castle laughed. "You have no need to seek farther," he said, "for the Green Knight dwells but a half-day's ride from here. Be my guest until the morning of New Year's Day, and then I will send you on your way."

Gawaine was overjoyed, for he had feared above all things that he might not be able to keep faith and be shamed for ever as a coward, and he thanked his host with gladness.

"Before you leave here," said the lord, "I would ask a favour of you."

"I shall do willingly anything you ask," said Gawaine.

"There are yet three days left to us before you need ride forth. You must still be wearied from your search; it would please me well if you would rest and take your ease for the next three days. Rise late and eat when you will, while I go hunting, and my lady shall stay with you to make you good cheer. And whatever I kill in the forest, it shall be a prize for you; if you will, for your part, give to me on my return any good fortune you have come by during the day." To this Gawaine gladly agreed.

The next morning the lord of the castle rode out early to hunt the stag, and Gawaine rose late and sat by the blazing fire talking to the lady of one thing and another.

But after a time the lady frowned a little and said, "Do you not find me fair, Sir Gawaine?"

"Indeed I do, lady," he replied.

Yet her frown deepened. "Indeed you do not," she said. "For never before have I talked so long with a Knight without his asking me to give him a kiss."

Now Gawaine would have thought shame to ask a lady for a kiss, even in jest, when her lord was not by, yet he did not wish to displease her nor would he have had her believe that he did not find her fair. "I would not fail in courtesy where other knights have not," he said.

And he rose and went to her and she kissed him, and straightway her frowns were gone and she smiled again, and they sat and talked further until, at evening, the lord of the castle returned.

In the hall he set out all the deer that he had killed, and a great number they were. "See what I have brought for you," he called to Gawaine. "Have I not done well today? Have you gained any good fortune to be compared with mine?"

"No more than this which I shall give to you," said Gawaine, and he kissed the lord of the castle.

The lord laughed mightily. "That is indeed sweet fortune," he said.

The next morning the lord of the castle rode out early to hunt the boar. As before, Gawaine rose late and sat by the blazing fire and talked with the lady of one thing and another. But as it drew near evening she frowned and said, "Sir Gawaine, do you no longer consider me fair? You have not asked me for a kiss today."

And in his courtesy Sir Gawaine rose and went to her, and she kissed him twice and her frowns were smoothed away and she smiled.

After a little while the lord of the castle returned, bringing with him the boar which he had slain. The boar's head he gave to Gawaine, saying, "See what I have gained today. Have you had any good fortune to compare with that?"

"No more than this which I give to you," said Gawaine, and he kissed his host twice.

The lord of the castle laughed loud and long. "Indeed," he said, "that was sweet fortune."

The next morning the lord of the castle rode out early to hunt the fox, and as before Sir Gawaine rose late and sat with the lady, and they talked of one thing and another. But as dusk was falling she frowned and said to him, "You are indeed a churlish knight, Sir Gawaine, that you have forgotten that yesterday you thought me fair. Today you have not asked me for a kiss."

And Gawaine rose and went to her, and she kissed him three times and her frowns vanished and she smiled. "Since you find me fair," she said, "will you not take a gift from me?" And she took off a jewelled ring she wore and held it out to him.

At first he did not know how to refuse her gift with courtesy, and then he said, "I thank you, lady, but I may not take such a costly gift from you when I have nothing to give you in return. I am here among strangers and all my goods are far away, so it would not be fitting that I should accept a ring from you and offer nothing in exchange."

"If it is only the value of the ring which troubles you, see, I will give you a gift that is of less worth." And she unfastened the long green girdle which she wore and held it out to him. "Let it be for a keepsake," she said.

But when he tried to refuse it, she smiled, "Poor gift though this girdle seems, it is not worthless. For any man who wears it is safe from death, and the blow of no weapon can harm him."

And Gawaine remembered how in no more than a few hours he would have to ride out to meet the Green Knight and withstand a blow from his mighty strength, and he was tempted and hesitated, looking on the green silken girdle that was embroidered with gold.

"Take it," pleaded the lady, "for that is my wish."

Gawaine took the girdle and thanked her; and at that moment they heard the baying of the hounds in the courtyard and the clatter of hoofs, and they knew that the lord of the castle was home.

Cheerily he called to Gawaine and gave him the skin of the fox with its white-tipped tail. "What good fortune have you gained today, my friend?" he asked.

"No more than this which I give to you." And Gawaine kissed him three times. But the girdle he hid and did not give to his host, for he knew that he would have great need of it on the morrow.

The lord of the castle threw back his head and his laughter

rang through the hall. "Indeed, that was sweet fortune," he said.

That evening they feasted merrily, and though it was Gawaine's last night at the castle there was much mirth and joy between them.

Before they went to rest, Gawaine thanked his host and the lady for all their courtesy. "I shall ever be grateful to you," he said.

Very early on New Year's Day Gawaine rode out from the castle, together with the squire whom the lord had bidden show him the way; and over his armour he wore the green girdle. They rode through a wood and up a hill, and then the squire pointed towards a tall rock that lay at a distance before them. "There, lord, is the cave where dwells the dread Green Knight. May all the saints protect you."

Gawaine thanked him and bade him farewell and rode on alone towards the rock, and when he came close he dismounted. Then he heard a mighty shout from above, and looking up, he saw the Green Knight, his head firmly on his shoulders, standing upon the rock, sharpening an axe on a whetstone.

The Green Knight leapt down from the rock and stood by him, towering and tall, a sight to bring fear even to the boldest of hearts. "You are welcome, Sir Gawaine," he said. "I am glad to learn that you are one who keeps faith. Now take off your helmet and let me strike my blow."

So Gawaine took off his helmet and bent his head to the axe, and the Green Knight raised his weapon high and brought it down mightily; but even as it fell, for all his courage, Gawaine shrank aside a little, and the Green Knight swerved his blow so that Gawaine was unharmed. "Indeed," said the Green Knight with scorn, "they told me that Sir Gawaine was among the bravest of all men and that he would quail at nothing. It seems that they were mistaken. Did you see me flinch when you struck your blow at me, last New Year's Day?"

"Strike again, Sir Green Knight, and this time I will not flinch, not even though my head falls in the snow. And unlike you I cannot pick it up and put it on my shoulders again." And Gawaine bent his head once more, trusting as much as he might in the girdle the lady had given him.

The Green Knight raised the axe again and brought it down in a mighty stroke, and this time Gawaine never stirred. But just as the axe would have touched his neck, the Green Knight stayed his hand and laughed. "Now that you have found your courage, it is time to strike my blow in earnest." And he raised the axe once more.

"You threaten too long," said Gawaine. "Strike and have done."

Gawaine and the Green Knight

A third time the Green Knight raised his axe and brought it down, but so skilfully did he wield it that it did no greater harm than he had intended, and broke no more than the skin of Gawaine's neck, so that a little blood trickled down upon the snow. And when Gawaine felt the blow and saw the blood, he leapt forward and snatched up his helmet and sword. "You have had your one blow, Sir Green Knight. If you would have another you will find it shall not go unreturned."

But the Green Knight leant upon his axe and laughed. "I have no quarrel with you, Sir Gawaine. I have given my one blow as promised, in fair exchange, and now is all discharged between us. The first blow which I would have struck you and did not strike was for the kiss you had of my lady and gave freely on to me. And the second time I threatened you was for the two kisses you had of her and restored. But when I struck you in earnest and wounded you, that was not for the three kisses which she gave you and which you rendered to me again, but for the green girdle which is mine and which you kept for yourself. For you must know that I am no other than the lord of the castle whose guest you have been these past seven days and more; and most welcome has your company been. My lady and I, as we decided between us, did but seek to try you with her kisses and my green girdle to see if you were a true knight or no, and well did you acquit yourself."

But Gawaine was ashamed. "It was my fear of death that made me keep the girdle. And it was that same cowardice that made me flinch from your stroke."

"It is but a little stain on so noble a knight, Sir Gawaine. There cannot be your like in all the land, and I am proud to have called you my friend. For I am indeed as you saw me at my castle and not as you see me now. This guise is but an enchantment put upon me by Queen Morgan le Fay, who is King Arthur's sister, for she wished to affright her brother and his knights of the Round Table. She believed that no one of them would dare to take up the challenge of a knight so huge and so fantastical as I when in the shape she gave me. Yet now is she proved wrong, and I am glad." And the Green Knight bade Gawaine return with him once more to his castle for further feasting and joy.

But Gawaine refused, saying, "I have been long away from King Arthur's court and I would return to them who perhaps grieve for me." He took off the green girdle and would have given it back, but the Green Knight prevented him. "It is no great gift for so rare a knight, for in truth it has no magic powers, but it is of my own lady's making, and I would that you kept it if it pleases you."

And Gawaine thanked him. "I will keep it to remind me of the moment when I failed in courage," he said. "And may it ever save me from further cowardice."

Then they embraced and Gawaine bade the Green Knight greet his lady for him, and mounting Gringolet, he rode on his way across the snow.

When he reached King Arthur's court once more, there was great rejoicing, for many had feared that he never would return to them. Much they wondered at the story which he had to tell them, and many there were who blamed the spite of Morgan le Fay. But all praised Sir Gawaine; and ever after the knights of the Round Table wore a girdle of green as a baldric to bear him company, and it was esteemed a great honour amongst them.

'Rikki-Tikki-Tavi'

————————————*————————————

At the hole where he went in
Red-Eye called to Wrinkled-Skin.
Hear what little Red-Eye saith
"Nag, come up and dance with death!"

Eye to eye and head to head,
(Keep the measure, Nag.)
This shall end when one is dead;
(At thy pleasure, Nag.)
Turn for turn, and twist for twist—
(Run and hide thee, Nag.)
Hah! The hooded Death has missed!
(Woe betide thee, Nag!)

This is the story of the great war that Rikki-tikki-tavi fought single-handed, through the bathrooms of the big bungalow in Segowlee cantonment. Darzee, the tailor-bird, helped him, and Chuchundra, the musk-rat, who never comes out into the middle of the floor, but always creeps round by the wall, gave him advice; but Rikki-tikki did the real fighting.

He was a mongoose, rather like a little cat in his fur and his

tail, but quite like a weasel in his head and his habits. His eyes
and the end of his restless nose were pink; he could scratch himself anywhere he pleased, with any leg, front or back, that he
chose to use; he could fluff up his tail till it looked like a bottle-
brush, and his war-cry, as he scuttled through the long grass,
was: "*Rikk-tikk-tikki-tikki-tchk!*"

One day, a high summer flood washed him out of the burrow
where he lived with his father and mother, and carried him,
kicking and clucking, down a road-side ditch. He found a little
wisp of grass floating there, and clung to it till he lost his senses.
When he revived, he was lying in the hot sun on the middle of a
garden path, very draggled indeed, and a small boy was saying:
"Here's a dead mongoose. Let's have a funeral."

"No," said his mother; "let's take him in and dry him.
Perhaps he isn't really dead."

They took him into the house, and a big man picked him up
between his finger and thumb, and said he was not dead but
half choked; so they wrapped him in cotton wool, and warmed
him, and he opened his eyes and sneezed.

"Now," said the big man (he was an Englishman who had
just moved into the bungalow); "don't frighten him and we'll
see what he'll do."

It is the hardest thing in the world to frighten a mongoose,
because he is eaten up from nose to tail with curiosity. The
motto of all the mongoose family is "Run and find out"; and
Rikki-tikki was a true mongoose. He looked at the cotton wool,
decided that it was not good to eat, ran all round the table, sat
up and put his fur in order, scratched himself, and jumped on
the small boy's shoulder.

"Don't be frightened, Teddy," said his father. "That's his
way of making friends."

"Ouch! He's tickling under my chin," said Teddy.

Rikki-tikki looked down between the boy's collar and neck,

174

snuffed at his ear, and climbed down to the floor, where he sat rubbing his nose.

"Good gracious," said Teddy's mother, "and that's a wild creature! I suppose he's so tame because we've been kind to him."

"All mongooses are like that," said her husband. "If Teddy doesn't pick him up by the tail, or try to put him in a cage, he'll run in and out of the house all day long. Let's give him something to eat."

They gave him a little piece of raw meat. Rikki-tikki liked it immensely, and when it was finished he went out into the veranda and sat in the sunshine and fluffed up his fur to make it dry to the roots. Then he felt better.

"There are more things to find out about in this house," he said to himself, "than all my family could find out in all their lives. I shall certainly stay and find out."

He spent all that day roaming over the house. He nearly drowned himself in the bath-tubs, put his nose into the ink on a writing-table and burnt it on the end of the big man's cigar, for he climbed up in the big man's lap to see how writing was done. At nightfall he ran into Teddy's nursery to watch how kerosene-lamps were lighted, and when Teddy went to bed Rikki-tikki climbed up too; but he was a restless companion, because he had to get up and attend to every noise all through the night, and find out what made it. Teddy's mother and father came in, the last thing, to look at their boy, and Rikki-tikki was awake on the pillow. "I don't like that," said Teddy's mother; "he may bite the child." "He'll do no such thing," said the father. "Teddy's safer with that little beast than if he had a bloodhound to watch him. If a snake came into the nursery now——"

But Teddy's mother wouldn't think of anything so awful.

Early in the morning Rikki-tikki came to early breakfast in the veranda riding on Teddy's shoulder, and they gave him

banana and some boiled egg; and he sat on all their laps one
after the other, because every well-brought-up mongoose always
hopes to be a house-mongoose some day and have rooms to run
about in, and Rikki-tikki's mother (she used to live in the
General's house at Segowlee) had carefully told Rikki what to
do if ever he came across white men.

Then Rikki-tikki went out into the garden to see what was to
be seen. It was a large garden, only half-cultivated, with bushes
as big as summer-houses of Marshal Niel roses, lime and orange
trees, clumps of bamboos, and thickets of high grass. Rikki-tikki
licked his lips. "This is a splendid hunting-ground," he said, and
his tail grew bottle-brushy at the thought of it, and he scuttled
up and down the garden, snuffing here and there till he heard
very sorrowful voices in a thorn-bush.

It was Darzee, the tailor-bird, and his wife. They had made a
beautiful nest by pulling two big leaves together and stitching
them up the edges with fibres, and had filled the hollow with
cotton and downy fluff. The nest swayed to and fro, as they sat
on the rim and cried.

"What is the matter?" asked Rikki-tikki.

"We are very miserable," said Darzee. "One of our babies
fell out of the nest yesterday, and Nag ate him."

"H'm!" said Rikki-tikki, "that is very sad—but I am a
stranger here. Who is Nag?"

Darzee and his wife only cowered down in the nest without
answering, for from the thick grass at the foot of the bush there
came a low hiss—a horrid cold sound that made Rikki-tikki
jump back two clear feet. Then inch by inch out of the grass
rose up the head and spread hood of Nag, the big black cobra,
and he was five feet long from tongue to tail. When he had lifted
one-third of himself clear of the ground, he stayed balancing to
and fro exactly as a dandelion-tuft balances in the wind, and he
looked at Rikki-tikki with the wicked snake's eyes that never

change their expression, whatever the snake may be thinking of.

"Who is Nag?" said he. "*I* am Nag. The great god Brahm put his mark upon all our people when the first cobra spread his hood to keep the sun off Brahm as he slept. Look, and be afraid!"

He spread out his hood more than ever, and Rikki-tikki saw the spectacle-mark on the back of it that looks exactly like the eye part of a hook-and-eye fastening. He was afraid for the minute; but it is impossible for a mongoose to stay frightened for any length of time, and though Rikki-tikki had never met a live cobra before, his mother had fed him on dead ones, and he knew that all a grown mongoose's business in life was to fight and eat snakes. Nag knew that too, and at the bottom of his cold heart he was afraid.

177

"Well," said Rikki-tikki, and his tail began to fluff up again, "marks or no marks, do you think it is right for you to eat fledglings out of a nest?"

Nag was thinking to himself, and watching the least little movement in the grass behind Rikki-tikki. He knew that mongooses in the garden meant death sooner or later for him and his family, but he wanted to get Rikki-tikki off his guard. So he dropped his head a little, and put it on one side.

"Let us talk," he said. "You eat eggs. Why should not I eat birds?"

"Behind you! Look behind you!" sang Darzee.

Rikki-tikki knew better than to waste time in staring. He jumped up in the air as high as he could go, and just under him whizzed by the head of Nagaina, Nag's wicked wife. She had crept up behind him as he was talking, to make an end of him; and he heard her savage hiss as the stroke missed. He came down almost across her back, and if he had been an old mongoose he would have known that then was the time to break her back with one bite; but he was afraid of the terrible lashing return-stroke of the cobra. He bit, indeed, but did not bite long enough, and he jumped clear of the whisking tail, leaving Nagaina torn and angry.

"Wicked, wicked Darzee!" said Nag, lashing up as high as he could reach towards the nest in the thorn-bush; but Darzee had built it out of reach of snakes, and it only swayed to and fro.

Rikki-tikki felt his eyes growing red and hot (when a mongoose's eyes grow red, he is angry), and he sat back on his tail and hind legs like a little kangaroo, and looked all round him, and chattered with rage. But Nag and Nagaina had disappeared into the grass. When a snake misses its stroke, it never says anything or gives any sign of what it means to do next. Rikki-tikki did not care to follow them, for he did not feel sure that he could manage two snakes at once. So he trotted off to the gravel path near the house, and sat down to think. It was a serious matter for him.

If you read the old books of natural history, you will find they say that when the mongoose fights the snake and happens to get bitten, he runs off and eats some herb that cures him. That is not true. The victory is only a matter of quickness of eye and quickness of foot—snake's blow against mongoose's jump—and as no eye can follow the motion of a snake's head when it strikes, that makes things much more wonderful than any magic herb. Rikki-tikki knew he was a young mongoose, and it made him all the more pleased to think that he had managed to escape a blow from behind. It gave him confidence in himself, and when Teddy came running down the path Rikki-tikki was ready to be petted.

But just as Teddy was stooping, something wriggled a little in the dust, and a tiny voice said: "Be careful. I am death!" It was Karait, the dusty brown snakeling that lies for choice on the dusty earth; and his bite is as dangerous as the cobra's. But he is so small that nobody thinks of him, and so he does the more harm to people.

Rikki-tikki's eyes grew red again, and he danced up to Karait with the peculiar rocking, swaying motion that he had inherited from his family. It looks very funny, but it is so perfectly balanced a gait that you can fly off it at any angle you please; and in dealing with snakes this is an advantage. If Rikki-tikki had only known, he was doing a much more dangerous thing than fighting Nag, for Karait is so small, and can turn so quickly, that unless Rikki bit him close to the back of the head he would get the return-stroke in his eye or lip. But Rikki did not know: his eyes were all red, and he rocked back and forth, looking for a good place to hold. Karait struck out. Rikki jumped sideways and tried to run in, but the wicked little dusty grey head lashed within a fraction of his shoulder, and he had to jump over the body, and the head followed his heels close.

Teddy shouted to the house: "Oh, look here! Our mongoose is killing a snake"; and Rikki-tikki heard a scream from Teddy's mother. His father ran out with a stick, but by the time he came up, Karait had lunged out once too far, and Rikki-tikki had sprung, jumped on the snake's back, dropped his head far between his forelegs, bitten as high up the back as he could get hold, and rolled away. That bite paralysed Karait, and Rikki-tikki was just going to eat him up from the tail, after the custom of his family at dinner, when he remembered that a full meal makes a slow mongoose, and if he wanted all his strength and quickness ready, he must keep himself thin.

He went away for a dust-bath under the castor-oil bushes, while Teddy's father beat the dead Karait. "What is the use of that?" thought Rikki-tikki. "I have settled it all"; and then Teddy's mother picked him up from the dust and hugged him, crying that he had saved Teddy from death, and Teddy's father said that he was a providence, and Teddy looked on with big scared eyes. Rikki-tikki was rather amused at all the fuss, which, of course, he did not understand. Teddy's mother might just as well have petted Teddy for playing in the dust. Rikki was thoroughly enjoying himself.

That night, at dinner, walking to and fro among the wine-glasses on the table, he might have stuffed himself three times over with nice things; but he remembered Nag and Nagaina, and though it was very pleasant to be patted and petted by Teddy's mother, and to sit on Teddy's shoulder, his eyes would get red from time to time, and he would go off into his long war-cry of "*Rikk-tikk-tikki-tikki-tchk!*"

Teddy carried him off to bed, and insisted on Rikki-tikki sleeping under his chin. Rikki-tikki was too well bred to bite or scratch, but as soon as Teddy was asleep he went off for his nightly walk round the house, and in the dark he ran up against Chuchundra, the musk-rat, creeping round by the wall.

Chuchundra is a broken-hearted little beast. He whimpers and cheeps all the night, trying to make up his mind to run into the middle of the room, but he never gets there.

"Don't kill me," said Chuchundra, almost weeping. "Rikki-tikki, don't kill me."

"Do you think a snake-killer kills musk-rats?" said Rikki-tikki scornfully.

"Those who kill snakes get killed by snakes," said Chuchundra, more sorrowfully than ever. "And how am I to be sure that Nag won't mistake me for you some dark night?"

"There's not the least danger," said Rikki-tikki; "but Nag is in the garden, and I know you don't go there."

"My cousin Chua, the rat, told me——" said Chuchundra, and then he stopped.

"Told you what?"

"H'sh! Nag is everywhere, Rikki-tikki. You should have talked to Chua in the garden."

"I didn't—so you must tell me. Quick, Chuchundra, or I'll bite you!"

Chuchundra sat down and cried till the tears rolled off his whiskers. "I am a very poor man," he sobbed. "I never had spirit enough to run out into the middle of the room. H'sh! I mustn't tell you anything. Can't you *hear*, Rikki-tikki?"

Rikki-tikki listened. The house was as still as still, but he thought he could just catch the faintest scratch-scratch in the world—a noise as faint as that of a wasp walking on a window-pane—the dry scratch of a snake's scales on brickwork.

"That's Nag or Nagaina," he said to himself; "and he is crawling into the bathroom sluice. You're right, Chuchundra; I should have talked to Chua."

He stole off to Teddy's bathroom, but there was nothing there, and then to Teddy's mother's bathroom. At the bottom of the smooth plaster wall there was a brick pulled out to make a sluice for the bath-water, and as Rikki-tikki stole in by the masonry curb where the bath is put, he heard Nag and Nagaina whispering together outside in the moonlight.

"When the house is emptied of people," said Nagaina to her husband, "he will have to go away, and then the garden will be our own again. Go in quietly, and remember that the big man who killed Karait is the first one to bite. Then come out and tell me, and we will hunt for Rikki-tikki together."

"But are you sure that there is anything to be gained by killing the people?" said Nag.

"Everything. When there were no people in the bungalow, did we have any mongoose in the garden? So long as the bungalow is empty, we are king and queen of the garden; and remember that as soon as our eggs in the melon-bed hatch (as they may tomorrow), our children will need room and quiet."

"I had not thought of that," said Nag. "I will go, but there is no need that we should hunt for Rikki-tikki afterward. I will kill the big man and his wife, and the child if I can, and come away quietly. Then the bungalow will be empty and Rikki-tikki will go."

Rikki-tikki tingled all over with rage and hatred at this, and then Nag's head came through the sluice, and his five feet of cold body followed it. Angry as he was, Rikki-tikki was very frightened as he saw the size of the big cobra. Nag coiled himself up, raised his head and looked into the bathroom in the dark, and Rikki could see his eyes glitter.

"Now, if I kill him here, Nagaina will know; and if I fight him on the open floor, the odds are in his favour. What am I to do?" said Rikki-tikki-tavi.

Nag waved to and fro, and then Rikki-tikki heard him drinking from the biggest water-jar that was used to fill the bath. "That is good," said the snake. "Now, when Karait was killed, the big man had a stick. He may have that stick still, but when he comes in to bathe in the morning he will not have a stick. I shall wait here till he comes. Nagaina—do you hear me?—I shall wait here in the cool till daytime."

There was no answer from outside, so Rikki-tikki knew Nagaina had gone away. Nag coiled himself down, coil by coil, round the bulge at the bottom of the water-jar, and Rikki-tikki stayed still as death. After an hour he began to move, muscle by muscle, towards the jar. Nag was asleep, and Rikki-tikki looked at his big back, wondering which would be the best place for a good hold. "If I don't break his back at the first jump," said Rikki, "he can still fight; and if he fights—O, Rikki!" He looked at the thickness of the neck below the hood, but that was too much for him; and a bite near the tail would only make Nag savage.

"It must be the head," he said at last; "the head above the hood; and when I am once there, I must not let go."

Then he jumped. The head was lying a little clear of the water-jar, under the curve of it; and, as his teeth met, Rikki braced his back against the bulge of the red earthenware to hold down the head. This gave him just one second's purchase, and he made the most of it. Then he was battered to and fro as a rat is shaken by a dog—to and fro on the floor, up and down, and round in great circles; but his eyes were red, and he held on as the body cart-whipped over the floor, upsetting the tin dipper and the soap-dish and the flesh-brush, and banged against the tin side of the bath. As he held he closed his jaws tighter and tighter, for he made sure he would be banged to death, and, for the honour of his family, he preferred to be found with his teeth locked. He was lizzy, aching, and felt shaken to pieces when something went off like a thunderclap just behind him; a hot wind knocked him senseless, and red fire singed his fur. The big man had been wakened by the noise, and had fired both barrels of a shotgun into Nag just behind the hood.

Rikki-tikki held on with his eyes shut, for now he was quite sure he was dead; but the head did not move, and the big man picked him up and said: "It's the mongoose again, Alice; the little chap has saved *our* lives now." Then Teddy's mother came in with a very white face, and saw what was left of Nag, and Rikki-tikki dragged himself to Teddy's bedroom and spent half the rest of the night shaking himself tenderly to find out whether he really was broken into forty pieces, as he fancied.

When morning came he was very stiff, but well pleased with his doings. "Now I have Nagaina to settle with, and she will be worse than five Nags, and there's no knowing when the eggs she spoke of will hatch. Goodness! I must go and see Darzee," he said.

Without waiting for breakfast, Rikki-tikki ran to the thorn-bush where Darzee was singing a song of triumph at the top of his voice. The news of Nag's death was all over the garden, for the sweeper had thrown the body on the rubbish-heap.

"Oh, you stupid tuft of feathers!" said Rikki-tikki angrily. "Is this the time to sing?"

"Nag is dead—is dead—is dead!" sang Darzee. "The valiant Rikki-tikki caught him by the head and held fast. The big man brought the bang-stick, and Nag fell in two pieces! He will never eat my babies again."

"All that's true enough; but where's Nagaina?" said Rikki-tikki, looking carefully round him.

"Nagaina came to the bathroom sluice and called for Nag," Darzee went on; "and Nag came out on the end of a stick—the sweeper picked him up on the end of a stick and threw him upon the rubbish-heap. Let us sing about the great, the red-eyed Rikki-tikki!" and Darzee filled his throat and ang.

"If I could get up to your nest, I'd roll all your babies out!" said Rikki-tikki. "You don't know when to do the right thing at the right time. You're safe enough in your nest there, but it's war for me down here. Stop singing a minute, Darzee."

"For the great, the beautiful Rikki-tikki's sake I will stop," said Darzee. "What is it, O Killer of the terrible Nag?"

"Where is Nagaina, for the third time?"

"On the rubbish-heap by the stables, mourning for Nag. Great is Rikki-tikki with the white teeth."

"Bother my white teeth! Have you ever heard where she keeps her eggs?"

"In the melon-bed, on the end nearest the wall, where the sun strikes nearly all day. She hid them there weeks ago."

"And you never thought it worth while to tell me? The end nearest the wall, you said?"

"Rikki-tikki, you are not going to eat her eggs?"

"Not eat exactly; no. Darzee, if you have a grain of sense you will fly off to the stables and pretend that your wing is broken, and let Nagaina chase you away to this bush. I must get to the melon-bed, and if I went there now she'd see me."

Darzee was a feather-brained little fellow who could never hold more than one idea at a time in his head; and just because he knew that Nagaina's children were born in eggs like his own, he didn't think at first that it was fair to kill them. But his wife was a sensible bird, and she knew that cobra's eggs meant young cobras later on; so she flew off from the nest, and left Darzee to keep the babies warm, and continue his song about the death of Nag. Darzee was very like a man in some ways.

She fluttered in front of Nagaina by the rubbish-heap, and cried out: "Oh, my wing is broken! The boy in the house threw a stone at me and broke it." Then she fluttered more desperately than ever.

Nagaina lifted up her head and hissed: "You warned Rikki-tikki when I would have killed him. Indeed and truly, you've chosen a bad place to be lame in." And she moved towards Darzee's wife, slipping along over the dust.

"The boy broke it with a stone!" shrieked Darzee's wife.

"Well, it may be some consolation to you when you're dead to know that I shall settle accounts with the boy. My husband lies on the rubbish-heap this morning, but before night the boy in the house will lie very still. What is the use of running away? I am sure to catch you. Little fool, look at me!"

Darzee's wife knew better than to do that, for a bird who looks at a snake's eyes gets so frightened that she cannot move. Darzee's wife fluttered on, piping sorrowfully, and never leaving the ground, and Nagaina quickened her pace.

Rikki-tikki heard them going up the path from the stables, and he raced for the end of the melon-patch near the wall. There, in the warm litter about the melons, very cunningly hidden, he found twenty-five eggs, about the size of a bantam's eggs, but with whitish skins instead of shells.

"I was not a day too soon," he said; for he could see the baby cobras curled up inside the skin, and he knew that the minute they were hatched they could each kill a man or a mongoose. He bit off the tops of the eggs as fast as he could, taking care to crush the young cobras, and turned over the litter from time to time to see whether he had missed any. At last there were only three eggs left, and Rikki-tikki began to chuckle to himself, when he heard Darzee's wife screaming:

"Rikki-tikki, I led Nagaina towards the house, and she has gone into the veranda, and—oh, come quickly—she means killing!"

Rikki-tikki smashed two eggs, and tumbled backward down the melon-bed with the third egg in his mouth, and scuttled to the veranda as hard as he could put foot to the ground. Teddy and his mother and father were there at early breakfast; but Rikki-tikki saw that they were not eating anything. They sat stone-still, and their faces were white. Nagaina was coiled up on the matting by Teddy's chair, within easy striking-distance of Teddy's bare leg, and she was swaying to and fro singing a song of triumph.

"Son of the big man that killed Nag," she hissed, "stay still. I am not ready yet. Wait a little. Keep very still, all you three. If you move I strike, and if you do not move I strike. Oh, foolish people, who killed my Nag!"

Teddy's eyes were fixed on his father, and all his father could do was to whisper: "Sit still, Teddy. You mustn't move. Teddy, keep still."

Then Rikki-tikki came up and cried: "Turn round, Nagaina; turn and fight!"

"All in good time," said she, without moving her eyes. "I will settle my account with *you* presently. Look at your friends,

Rikki-tikki. They are still and white; they are afraid. They dare not move, and if you come a step nearer I strike."

"Look at your eggs," said Rikki-tikki, "in the melon-bed near the wall. Go and look, Nagaina."

The big snake turned half round, and saw the egg on the veranda. "Ah-h! Give it to me," she said.

Rikki-tikki put his paws one on each side of the egg, and his eyes were blood-red. "What price for a snake's egg? For a young cobra? For a young king-cobra? For the last—the very last of the brood? The ants are eating all the others down by the melon-bed."

Nagaina spun clear round, forgetting everything for the sake of the one egg; and Rikki-tikki saw Teddy's father shoot out a big hand, catch Teddy by the shoulder, and drag him across the little table with the teacups, safe and out of reach of Nagaina.

"Tricked! Tricked! Tricked! *Rikk-tck-tck!*" chuckled Rikki-tikki. "The boy is safe, and it was I—I—I that caught Nag by the hood last night in the bathroom." Then he began to jump up and down, all four feet together, his head close to the floor. "He threw me to and fro, but he could not shake me off. He was dead before the big man blew him in two. I did it. *Rikki-tikki-tck-tck!* Come then, Nagaina. Come and fight with me. You shall not be a widow long."

Nagaina saw that she had lost her chance of killing Teddy, and the egg lay between Rikki-tikki's paws. "Give me the egg, Rikki-tikki. Give me the last of my eggs, and I will go away and never come back," she said lowering her hood.

"Yes, you will go away, and you will never come back; for you will go on the rubbish-heap with Nag. Fight, widow! The big man has gone for his gun! Fight!"

Rikki-tikki was bounding all round Nagaina, keeping just out of reach of her stroke, his little eyes like hot coals. Nagaina gathered herself together, and flung out at him. Rikki-tikki jumped up and backwards. Again and again and again she struck, and each time her head came with a whack on the matting of the veranda, and she gathered herself together like a watch-spring. Then Rikki-tikki danced in a circle to get behind her, and Nagaina spun round to keep her head to his head, so that the rustle of her tail on the matting sounded like dry leaves blown along by the wind.

He had forgotten the egg. It still lay on the veranda, and Nagaina came nearer and nearer to it, till at last, while Rikki-tikki was drawing breath, she caught it in her mouth, turned to the veranda steps, and flew like an arrow down the path, with Rikki-tikki behind her. When the cobra runs for her life, she goes like a whiplash flicked across a horse's neck.

Rikki-tikki knew that he must catch her, or all the trouble would begin again. She headed straight for the long grass by the thorn-bush, and as he was running Rikki-tikki heard Darzee still singing his foolish little song of triumph. But Darzee's wife was wiser. She flew off her nest as Nagaina came along, and flapped her wings about Nagaina's head. If Darzee had helped they might have turned her; but Nagaina only lowered her hood and went on. Still, the instant's delay brought Rikki-tikki up to her, and as she plunged into the rat-hole where she and Nag used to live, his little white teeth were clenched on her tail, and he went down with her—and very few mongooses, however wise and old they may be, care to follow a cobra into its hole. It was dark in the hole; and Rikki-tikki never knew when it might open out and give Nagaina room to turn and strike at him. He held on savagely, and struck out his feet to act as brakes on the dark slope of the hot, moist earth.

Then the grass by the mouth of the hole stopped waving, and Darzee said: "It is all over with Rikki-tikki! We must sing his death-song. Valiant Rikki-tikki is dead! For Nagaina will surely kill him underground."

So he sang a very mournful song that he made up on the spur of the minute, and just as he got to the most touching part the grass quivered again, and Rikki-tikki, covered with dirt, dragged himself out of the hole leg by leg, licking his whiskers. Darzee stopped with a little shout. Rikki-tikki shook some of the dust out of his fur and sneezed. "It is all over," he said. "The widow will never come out again." And the red ants that live between the grass-stems heard him, and began to troop down one after another to see if he had spoken the truth.

Rikki-tikki curled himself up in the grass and slept where he was—slept and slept till it was late in the afternoon, for he had done a hard day's work.

"Now," he said, when he awoke, "I will go back to the house. Tell the Coppersmith, Darzee, and he will tell the garden that Nagaina is dead."

The Coppersmith is a bird who makes a noise exactly like the beating of a little hammer on a copper pot; and the reason he is always making it is because he is the town-crier to every Indian garden, and tells all the news to everybody who cares to listen. As Rikki-tikki went up the path, he heard his "attention" notes like a tiny dinner-gong; and then the steady, "*Ding-dong-tock!* Nag is dead—*dong!* Nagaina is dead! *Ding-dong-tock!*" That set all the birds in the garden singing, and the frogs croaking; for Nag and Nagaina used to eat frogs as well as little birds.

When Rikki got to the house, Teddy and Teddy's mother (she looked very white still, for she had been fainting) and Teddy's father came out and almost cried over him; and that night he ate all that was given him till he could eat no more, and went to bed on Teddy's shoulder, where Teddy's mother saw him when she came to look late at night.

"He saved our lives and Teddy's life," she said to her husband. "Just think, he saved all our lives!"

Rikki-tikki woke up with a jump, for the mongooses are light sleepers.

"Oh, it's you," said he. "What are you bothering for? All the cobras are dead; and if they weren't, I'm here."

Rikki-tikki had a right to be proud of himself; but he did not grow too proud, and he kept that garden as a mongoose should keep it, with tooth and jump and spring and bite, till never a cobra dared show its head inside the walls.